WHEN A STAR HAS FALLEN

Stacey Walker

Dedication

In Loving Memory of Marvin Vaughn Jr.
Your light walked with me through every page.
Though your star has risen beyond sight,
its warmth remains: guiding, steady, and true.
This book is for you.

Book Review

Wow! 🏛 What an absolutely stunning book! I'm not usually a big reader, but I was completely drawn in—I loved it! I could see every character so clearly, and I didn't want it to end.
And that ending...what a beautiful, powerful invitation! 🏆🏛🎉 Congratulations! I'm so excited for others to experience this incredible story.
— Kathryn Nicoll, Gallatin, TN

A Note to the Reader

Dear Reader,

If this story spoke to your soul, I hope you'll share that experience with someone else. Whether it's a conversation, a prayer, or a posted review, your voice can help this message reach others who need to hear it.

✨ Leave a review.

📖 Share the story.

💬 Let the light keep traveling.

Thank you for reading. You matter more than you know.

—Stacey

READER'S GUIDE

How to Use This Guide

This guide is designed to help you reflect deeply on the themes of identity, rebellion, redemption, and purpose found throughout *When a Star Has Fallen*.

The story is written in a poetic and symbolic style, with echoes of C.S. Lewis's imaginative storytelling. You may notice British-style spellings or turns of phrase—these are intentional, adding to the timeless, otherworldly quality of the book.

Each chapter invites contemplation. Some characters represent concepts. Others evolve with surprising humanity. As you read, don't rush. Linger. Ask questions. Wonder. There are hidden threads meant to be uncovered with time.

- Pause at the end of each chapter to reflect.
- Journal insights or reactions.
- Use the questions below for group discussion or personal exploration.
- If you're mentoring a younger reader, use the questions to spark deeper conversation.

Questions to Reflect On Throughout the Book

1. Loka's journey mirrors a tragic fall. At what point do you believe his path was sealed? Was there a moment of no return?

2. Sin Say is both wounded and wounding. What do you make of his motives? Does he truly care for Loka or for power?

3. Goodwin represents harmony. How do you see his influence working behind the scenes?

4. Christian appears rarely, but always powerfully. What does this say about how the Son works in the real world?

5. The Place Called Beautiful is more than a setting. What emotions or longings did it stir in you?

6. The creatures, Grace, Mercy, Liberty, and Syracuse, blend humour and gravity. Which one most surprised or moved you?

7. The battle before time is not fought with death, but with binding. How does this reshape your understanding of spiritual warfare?

8. Redemption and rebellion are intertwined. What do you think the story teaches about pride and the possibility of restoration?

Final Thought

This is a story for the heart and the spirit. Some truths lie beneath the surface, waiting to be discovered. You're not just reading *When a Star Has Fallen*; you're walking a path where beauty and brokenness meet, and where redemption is still possible.

OPENING REFLECTION

Why Is There Evil?

One of the most powerful answers I've encountered to the question, *"Why did God create evil?"* comes from a story involving a university professor and a student.

The professor challenged his class:

"If God created everything, He must have created evil. Doesn't that make God evil?"

The class fell silent until one student spoke up.

"Professor, does cold exist?"

"Of course," the professor replied.

"No, sir," the student said. "Cold is only the absence of heat. We don't measure cold itself—just how little heat is present. The same goes for darkness—it's the absence of light."

The student continued:

"Evil is not a created thing, but the absence of God—just as darkness is the absence of light, and cold the absence of heat. God didn't create evil; it appears where His presence is missing."

And the story goes that the professor had no reply.

That student's name, **according to tradition, was Albert Einstein.**

Poem

When a Star Has Fallen
Who knows his story,
what it must have felt like
at the height of its glory?
All the things he must have seen
at the dawn of the age—
watching the world's story written
page by page.
The best and brightest
he must have been—
until pride took over
and sin crept in.
What a tragedy for all to see—
he was thrown from the heights,
into outer darkness,
and the edge of the night.
To ascend no more,
no purpose or calling...
Everyone experiences sadness
when a star has fallen.

Preface

There are moments when someone you trust, someone you believe will guide you through life's hardest seasons, suddenly falls. It's not a stumble; it's a collapse, and the impact isn't easily contained. It shakes your faith, your community, and even your sense of self. I've seen this unraveling firsthand. Maybe you have too.

When a Star Has Fallen was born out of that space: the painful tension between what we expect and what reality delivers when the unthinkable happens.

The characters in this story are fictional, but their emotions are not. Confusion, betrayal, silence, these are real experiences many of us carry, often in secret. I wrote this story to give shape to those feelings and to offer a way forward when the path ahead seems impossible.

This isn't just a story about loss. It's about the aftermath; the questions that rise in the rubble: *Can I trust again? What does it mean to believe now? Can I move on?*

As you read, you'll walk with characters who wrestle with these very questions. The fall of someone we looked to for guidance doesn't mean the end of the journey. Sometimes it marks the beginning of a deeper, more personal path to healing.

The questions you'll encounter here aren't simple. But they're the questions that lead to growth. Trust, faith, hope, all these things can live again, even after the deepest wounds.

I invite you to join this journey not to indulge in sorrow, but to find restoration. Bring your doubts, your brokenness, your questions. My hope is that somewhere within these pages, you'll see the light not in the fallen leader, but in the One who never falls.

—Stacey Walker

Introduction

Fictional Story, Real Impact

There's a unique kind of silence that follows the fall of someone we once admired: a leader, a mentor, a friend. It's not just the sound of disappointment. It's the ache of disillusionment. We ask: *How could someone so steady lose their way? And what are we supposed to do now?*

This book isn't about blame. It's about healing. It's for those left in the aftermath; the ones who trusted, followed, or were inspired, but now feel confused, hurt, even angry. It's about walking through the wreckage of broken trust and spiritual exhaustion when someone who once pointed us to Jesus loses sight of Him.

The characters are fictional, but the emotions are not. The pain, the betrayal, the grief, they're real for many who've watched their heroes fall. This story doesn't call out any scandal. Instead, it explores the spiritual and emotional impact left behind. Because when a star falls, the tremors reach everyone who once drew strength from its light.

At its core, *When a Star Has Fallen* is rooted in biblical truth, drawing insight from the NKJV Remnant Study Bible. Out of those foundations comes a style I call *fantasy realism*: a blend of imagination and reality that invites you into a deeper understanding of spiritual struggle.

This story draws us into the ancient conflict between good and evil, a battle older than humanity itself. At the center is Loka, the Day Star, once radiant and honored, now burdened by pride. Through his journey, we see the tragedy of a being created for beauty and purpose who chose to crave the light for himself.

This isn't a conventional religious tale. It's an invitation to imagine, to empathize, and to feel. You may laugh with the characters, grieve with them, or even see yourself in them. The themes—pride, power, disillusionment, redemption—echo across cultures and centuries.

We celebrate when leaders rise, but we are devastated when they fall. That cycle of ascent and collapse is what this book's title captures: *When a Star Has Fallen.*

And yet, beyond every collapse lies a question:

Is there life beyond this? Beyond the failure, beyond the fracture, beyond what we thought we knew about God, people, and ourselves?

This book doesn't give easy answers. But it offers a place to begin again; to ask better questions, to feel honestly, and to look higher than the fallen. Because while stars may fall, they cannot dim the eternal light of the One who still holds the heavens, and our hearts, in place.

CHAPTER ONE

The Music Before the Morning

In the beginning, before time first stirred in its cradle, before light unfolded her golden wings across the void, there was a Song.

Not a song as mortals know it, born from throats or pressed into parchment, but a deep, resonant harmony that breathed life into the unformed and traced the borders of reality.

It was not bound by melody or measure, yet it moved with purpose. Its sound was like rivers of light flowing through caverns of shadow, like winds racing over oceans of glass, like fire that warmed without burning.

It was the language of the One, and all that would ever exist was hidden within its notes. When the Song swelled, stars bloomed. When it softened, worlds gathered in their orbits. Every pulse, every vibration, carried the heartbeat of the Creator.

In that first, perfect music, there was no dissonance—only harmony so pure that even silence seemed alive.

From this primordial Music came three great and eternal beings, as old as reality itself and untouched by decay or death. Their names are not easily spoken in the tongues of time-bound creatures, but we may call them Goodwin, Sin Say, and the Creator.

With them was Christian, the Son of the Creator, begotten, not made, co-eternal with His Father, the Word through whom the Song itself flowed.

These were no mere figures of light and shadow, but persons, real, potent, and endlessly mysterious. They did not come into being; they simply were, and ever shall be.

THE FIRST TENSION

Goodwin, fair and wise, moved with a presence that stilled the storms of newborn stars. When he passed among them, the raging clouds of flame bent low, hushed like children soothed by a father's hand. Even the lightning grew quiet, folding itself back into rivers of fire at his bidding.

He was the Breath that brought balance, the Thought that ordered chaos, the Hand that restored what was broken. When he sang, the Song's harmony deepened, and creation leaned in to listen.

Beside him, for ages uncounted, walked his brother-in-form, Sin Say.

Once, Sin Say's voice shone like crystal light, carrying joy through the heavens. His notes danced with Goodwin's, weaving beauty too vast for mortal eyes.

But the beauty was not enough.

It began subtly, an almost imperceptible hesitation in his harmonies, a glance toward the throne where the Creator sat.

In the midst of shaping a new world, its oceans gleaming with silver light, Sin Say paused. His gaze lingered, not on the world they were crafting, but on the authority from which it came.

If I led, would not the Song rise higher? The thought slipped in like a shadow. He pictured the stars leaning toward him, their light answering his alone. He imagined the galaxies turning at his gesture, worlds aligning at his command.

"Why," he murmured in a tone so low it trembled in the space between moments, "should the Song not be mine to lead?"

Goodwin's answering chord was steady, but there was a strain in it. "Because it was never ours to begin with."

The hesitation hardened into resolve.

Sin Say's next note clashed, not by accident, but by will. It was sharp, discordant, slicing through the harmony like a blade.

The shock rippled through the heavens; creatures turned their heads, stars quivered in their courses. That single, deliberate dissonance was the seed of rebellion.

His fall was not a stumble but a defiance.

With a voice now filled with thunder and venom, he tore himself from the harmony of love and declared his own dreadful motif. From this defiance was born Evil, not as a thing created, but as a parasite, a twisting of what had been good.

OF THE CREATOR AND HIS SON

The Creator, He whom all things echo but none can fully behold, watched.

Not with surprise, for nothing surprises the One who stands outside of time. His gaze was steady, unshaken, for the Song was His, and no discord could undo what He had purposed.

Beside Him was Christian, His radiant Son, the bridge between the eternal and the created.

Where Christian walked, galaxies lifted their voices in response. Stars burned brighter in His nearness, and entire constellations bent themselves into choruses of praise. Nebulae unfurled like banners at His passing, their colors shifting into songs visible as light.

He would pass among the worlds like a gardener among flowers, speaking joy into their roots, drawing laughter from their skies.

He was the Word made visible, the melody in flesh, the living promise that no shadow would have the final verse.

Together, Father and Son did not recoil from Sin Say's rebellion. Instead, they began something more wonderful still: redemption.

The Creator does not conquer through coercion but woos with wonder. He is no tyrant of the stars but the Father of worlds. Where Sin Say would force, the Creator invites. Where Sin Say devours, the Creator nourishes.

In His design, even the darkness—yes, even the rebellion—is woven into a greater beauty.

THE LEAGUE OF NATIONS

Across the heavens, the Creator sowed worlds like seeds in a boundless garden.

There was Elorin, a world whose seas shimmered with liquid sapphire and whose skies bloomed with auroras that sang in colors. On its shores, waves struck the rocks with a sound like choirs rising, and travelers swore they could taste music in the salt wind.

There was Veyrah, where mountains were crowned in living crystal and the rivers carried songs downstream to the valleys.

And there was Thal-Mor, a realm of wind-borne cities where beings with wings of light traded stories as currency.

These worlds, though beyond human imagining, shared one truth: they were bound by love to the Creator. Not by fear, not by domination, but by a deep, willing joy.

This was the League of Nations: not a treaty, but a communion. Each swore allegiance not with ink and seal, but with trust and devotion.

Under Goodwin's guidance and Christian's light, they flourished.

Yet at the edges of these bright realms, shadows gathered. A whispered rumor here. A seed of pride there. Sin Say's influence was subtle but certain, like frost creeping across a windowpane in the dead of night.

THE WAR BENEATH THE STARS

It is not a war fought only with armies, though there are such, or with blades, though swords have clashed.

It is a war of truth against falsehood, of light against shadow, of song against noise.

In the halls of the League's great council, ambassadors argued with a heat that was not their own, their words sharpened by unseen whispers. One rose trembling with anger, denouncing another as though a friend had become an enemy overnight. Others watched in stunned silence, not knowing the discord was born from a voice they could not hear.

In the skies above Elorin, two great messengers of light crossed blades, their clash scattering sparks like falling stars.

On Thal-Mor, a temple's sacred song faltered mid-verse as a single discord swept through the choir.

Sin Say's chaos is loud, brash, and convincing to the impatient ear.

But Goodwin's melody remains, the deeper, older song that undergirds all being. Those who hear it are changed. They rise to join the harmony, their voices strengthening the music that will one day silence all discord.

And so the story continues.

Some call it myth. Some call it mere allegory.

But there are those wise ones who know better.

They know the stars are not silent. They know the war is real.

And they await the day when Christian, Son of the Creator, will rise in glory, and the final verse of the great Song will be sung.

On that day, even Sin Say will bow.

A GLIMPSE BEFORE WE ENTER

If you skipped the map, stop here. Go back and look. That drawing is not decoration. It's not wallpaper to flip past. It's a door. A key. A glimpse. Every line and river, every tower and garden, whispers of something real. The Place Called Beautiful is not merely geography; it is memory. A promise our souls recognize, even if our minds can't name it yet. Look long enough at that map, and you may feel a tug as though you've been there before, in dreams or prayers. It is more than a chart of land. It is a prophecy etched in ink. A reminder that what is coming is more solid, more lasting, more glorious than the world we know. So, if your eyes slid past it, turn back. Trace the edges. Let wonder be your compass. Because what you are about to read will spring from those lines. That map is your first invitation.

Now, with your bearings in place, let us step inside.

CHAPTER TWO

The Place Called Beautiful

(Adapted from Revelation 21:1–4, 10–27)

There is a place, though I should warn you, you'll never find it with a compass or a clever phone, that floats somewhere beyond stars, planets, and the rather quarrelsome clocks of Earth. You might guess it lies east of the Milky Way or west of Andromeda, but you'd be wrong both times, and badly out of breath if you tried walking there.

It isn't a place you can visit. Not yet. It isn't even a place where time behaves. Time, in fact, gave up on this land ages ago and stomped off in protest, muttering to itself.

This is the realm where the Creator—yes, that Creator, not the bedtime-storybook one with a snowdrift beard, but the roaring, radiant, real One—reigns eternally. Not with scepter or velvet throne, but with a smile that splits the sky and eyes that see all things rightly. This place is His masterpiece. His laughter made solid.

Human eyes have never seen it, and if they did, they'd likely try to pave it, tax it, or name it something dreary like "Heaven Zone One." But let us not be cynical. Let us look.

ATMOSPHERE ALIVE

The land is saturated with beauty of the sort that makes your heart sit down for a moment and whisper, "Well now. I never knew." It's more real than anything you've touched, more dazzling than any poster or painted rainbow, more lovely than the best dream you ever forgot by morning.

The air hums. Not with noise, but with song. Not sung by choirs (though they join in), but by the atmosphere itself, as though the very molecules rejoice. They sing of the Creator's glory, the endless joy of being. Sometimes, I suspect, they even sing of how pleased they are with the color of themselves that day.

The weather? Perfect. But not "hotel air-conditioning" perfect. This is the kind of perfect that makes your lungs glad to be lungs. One breath feels like your soul has been dipped in lemon zest and polished with starlight.

COLORS AND SKY

Colors here defy catalogues. Rainbows don't simply appear; they frolic, laughing across the sky like overconfident butterflies, smearing nonsense across the firmament until even physicists throw up their hands.

The sky does not simply hang overhead; it performs. It swirls and dances through palettes so rich even angels lose their place in the choir. No sunrises or sunsets divide time, only endless wonder, shifting like a child's laughter that hides a secret.

WATERS THAT SPEAK

Step softly to the edge of Lake Beautiful. Don't be alarmed if the water compliments you; it does that. Its surface is clear as polished thought, and when the sky leans down to kiss it, the lake becomes a mirror of joy, scattering diamonds like nods of greeting.

Flowing through it is the River of Life, though that's only its travel name. Its true name can't be spoken unless your soul is tuned like a harp. The river never dries, never slows, never loses its shimmer. It carries renewal the way bees carry gold: effortlessly, generously.

Beyond lies the Sea of Forgiveness. Its glow is gentle, but its depth is older than sorrow. Still as moonlight, lit like holy embers, it doesn't just wash hands. It cleanses regret. Step into its waters, and burdens dissolve like shadows at noon.

FOREST AND TOWERS

Then comes Leafy Green, a forest so lush it might sprout wings and fly if not for its roots. The trees here are towering, their leaves as wide as loaves of bread, nourishing not just flesh but dignity. Their veins carry healing, not like medicine, but restoration of soul.

The forest is not silent. It murmurs, chuckles, even sings when the light hits right. The trees sway, not from wind, but from the breath of the Creator Himself. Even the grass has learned manners; it bows in praise. Stones hum a bass note of adoration.

Beyond them rise the Strong High Towers, mountains that do not loom but sing. Their presence declares: Here reigns Peace. Here dwells Joy. They are undisturbed, undiminished.

At their feet, wildflowers bloom with a stubborn radiance. They do not wilt. They do not apologize. They shine.

CREATURES OF WONDER

And then—ah, the creatures.

Four winged lions stand at the realm's corners, their wings stretched wide like banners of light. They are fierce, yet not cruel guardians whose roars sound more like hymns than threats. In quiet hours, they recite poetry to one another, voices carrying across the heavens like golden trumpets. One, they say, once adopted a wandering moonbeam and named it Nigel. Their watch is tireless, their joy unshaken. The borders they guard are not fences but thresholds of glory.

Above all soars Liberty, the eagle with four wings and seven eyes. Try not to stare; it makes her self-conscious. Her cry is not menace but majesty: a declaration that all wrongs will be made right. She is justice with feathers.

Unicorns with seven horns roam here. Turtles fly politely. Deer glance with forgiveness in their eyes for sins you haven't confessed yet. Each creature is marvel, as though the Creator whispered, "Let's have fun with this one."

And there is Syracuse the dragon. Wise, witty, fond of cocoa and riddles. Large, scaly, and terribly good at cheering people up. Once, they say, he made a weeping seraph laugh until she snorted sparks. He is not merely a guardian, but a friend.

THE CITY ITSELF

And now, the City.

It is what every earthly city longs to be and never is. Not built for conquest, but for return. It waits not for spaceships, but for a far older, better unveiling.

The city is vast: fifteen hundred miles wide, long, and high. Square as a jeweler's box, luminous as starlight caught in gold. Its walls rise not from fear but glory. Its gates, each a single pearl large enough for an army to march through. Its foundations glitter with gems no jeweler could price. Its streets shine like transparent gold, as if solid light had decided to be walkable. Even shadows here glow.

At the center flows the river from the throne of the Creator. Beside it stands the Tree of Life, fruit glowing with eternity, flavoring joy into every bite. Its leaves do not wither. They heal. They forgive. They sing lullabies to the soul.

INVITATION

And this, dear reader —yes, you—is the Place Called Beautiful.

Do not be surprised if it calls to you later. If your dreams begin to look more like this. If your heart skips when you see a rainbow, or hear a stream laugh, or feel the rustle of an old wise tree. You may already be halfway there.

This is where our story begins.

FINAL SEAL

Do not forget this glimpse, dear reader. Beauty is not a luxury here; it is a compass. What you have seen will return when shadows fall, like a lantern reminding you of home. Every trial in the story ahead, every question that shakes the heart, will be measured against the memory of this Place Called Beautiful. Hold it close, for even in the darkest chapters, this light will not be lost.

CHAPTER THREE

The Intruder

As remembered by an old whisper in the dark.

There are some characters so ancient and so familiar that, though you may not remember when you first heard of them, you can be sure they remember you. This one does not arrive with galloping hooves or blaring trumpets. No, he comes in silence. The kind that makes you check your pockets for something missing, like innocence or the last biscuit.

He has many names (don't they always?), but for our purposes, we'll call him what he calls himself: Sin Say.

"Sin is my given name," he boasts, as if monogrammed on a handkerchief. "And Say is the family I come from. You might say my reputation precedes me or trails behind me like smoke, depending on the wind."

He fancies himself clever, this shadowy speaker. He walks with the air of one not invited but comfortably settled on the good sofa. He doesn't creak the floorboards or slam doors; he simply is, like a draft in a locked room.

THE BOAST

"I've been locked in a grand quarrel with my brother Goodwin for ages untold," he declares to no one in particular, though his voice curls into corners like it hopes to be overheard. "Naturally, the Creator prefers him. Teachers' pets always do win the applause."

He chuckles, as though the memory of celestial rivalry amuses him. "Goodwin? Hah. Always tidy, always quoting truth like a schoolboy with perfect penmanship. And me? I color outside the lines."

"Truth without imagination," he mutters, "is a cage. I prefer the open door."

Now, here's where you must pay attention.

This imposter is no brute. Brutes are easy to spot and easier to block. But he? He whispers. He suggests. He persuades. He is not god, nor angel, nor man; he is quite content to remain something else. Something in-between. Not light. Not quite shadow. More like smoke that thinks.

"Unlike atoms," he says with pride, "I don't split things. I suggest they split themselves. And they usually do."

HIS TARGETS

He doesn't seek the clumsy or cruel. No, he seeks the bright-eyed, the noble, the eager. The ones who want so badly to do good, they forget to be wise. His chosen hosts are rarely found in sewers, but in temples, in dreams, and in halls of ambition.

"Find me an honest fellow who is just a pinch too proud of being honest," he says, wagging a spectral finger, "and I'll have him tripping over his own halo before the week is out."

And so it is here, in the Place Called Beautiful, a city not built of stone, but of intention, that his plan begins to thicken, like cream left too long in lukewarm tea.

THE SEAT OF GLORY

The Capital is no ordinary realm. It is the seat of interplanetary governance, where the federations of worlds bend their knee to the Creator. At its center, the Hall of Lights, a name that echoes with trumpets and scales and glory at dawn.

There, the Creator sits. Not robed in fashion, but in glory. And beside Him, the Son, Christian, they call Him. They do not rule by law alone, but by love. A love so luminous it dazzles honest souls and makes dishonest ones sick to their stomachs.

"Yuck," mutters Sin Say. "All that glory and goodness. It's enough to give a fellow indigestion."

But still...he watches.

A TARGET TOO BRIGHT

Among the flame-eyed, thunder-winged hosts, those who speak in chords and walk on clouds, there is one who catches the intruder's eye. A bright one. Too bright, perhaps.

His name is Loka, the Day Star. Most radiant of the host. Draped in jewels, cloaked in splendor, walking not only among flowers, but among fire-stones. His dwelling, the Edenic Garden, lies near the Creator's mountain. And what's more, he is loved. Deeply. Called son not in jest, but in solemn truth.

Most would tread lightly around such a being. But not Sin Say. He does not see beauty to be revered, but a ladder to climb. And what better rung than the highest?

DIALOGUE WITH HIMSELF

"Loka," he croons in rehearsal, "my bright and perfect prospect. The crown jewel of the Creator's collection. You have everything except the one thing I can give: me."

He pauses, tasting the words. "Hmm. No, too forward. Needs more flattery."

He adjusts his tone, soft as spilled oil. "Oh radiant one, why should you, of all beings, not sit closer to the throne? Surely the Creator has more to give, and surely you deserve more."

"Closer...yes, that's the word. Who doesn't want to be closer? Closer to glory, closer to power, closer to being indispensable."

He chuckles at his own craft. "Yes, appeal to his brightness. Turn admiration into entitlement. Every angel wants to be useful; I'll convince him he ought to be indispensable."

He smirks, straightening what is not a collar. "I'm not here to storm the walls. I'm here to hand him a crown, invisible, but heavy enough to bend him toward me."

Then, mocking Goodwin, he adds with a sneer: "Duty, discipline, devotion. Ha! Let him keep his tidy lessons. Loka wants destiny. And I know how to spell it in letters of fire."

THE ALMOST BEAUTIFUL MADE CROOKED

You may shudder. You're meant to. For it is not the grotesque that is most frightening, but the almost-beautiful made crooked.

Sin Say imagines himself playing chess with the Maker. What he doesn't see is that the final move was played before the board was built. But evil always insists on making its move, even when the game is lost.

"People say evil wears red and carries a pitchfork. Nonsense. I wear silk; ideas woven into words and served on silver platters. People always swallow what's well-presented."

He smirks again, tugging on invisible cuffs. "And if they choke? I'll call it their choice."

TIME AND ENVY

"They say I have an expiration date. That time will eventually snuff me out like an old lamp. Ha! Let the gossips gossip. I've done rather well without their calendar."

He would never admit it, but envy is a fathering instinct too. It adopts in order to destroy.

"Yes," he whispers, dark eyes gleaming. "Today, I shall become his father, and he shall be my son. Unbeknownst to Loka the Day Star, today, he takes my hand."

He lets the thought linger, savoring it like a fine wine. "And once envy enters, it never leaves quietly."

EXIT LINES

He straightens. If such a being can straighten.

"I must go," he says, standing not quite on legs, and not quite standing. "There is work to be done in the Place Called Beautiful.

My quarry awaits. My hour draws near."

He lingers, savoring the sound of his own voice. "They say every dog has his day. I prefer the term predator. Less...domestic."

And then, with one last whisper, "People imagine I shout or scream or sing profane songs. I don't. I whisper. That's the secret. No one sins loudly. Only deliberately."

And he vanished as quietly as ink in water.

THE WARNING

And somewhere, perhaps in the city's garden, or the Hall of Lights, or in the uncertain silence between thoughts, a leaf began to fall.

Not dead. Not yet. But as if it had been warned.

CHAPTER FOUR

Love, That Immortal Flame

Sin Say's last whisper still lingered in the air: "No one sins loudly. Only deliberately."

But whispers, however slick, do not have the final word. For every shadow has its counterpoint. And where smoke curls, flame endures.

And so, let us speak not first of Sin, but of Love.

LOVE, THAT IMMORTAL FLAME

In a universe so immense that mortal thought can scarcely imagine its outlines without running aground in confusion, one reality ruled without rival or rivaling shadow: Love.

Not love as humans often mean it—a warm feeling prone to fade by morning—but Love in its most ancient and blazing form. Love that is. Love that sings, governs, binds, builds, gives, and never takes. Love not as sentiment, but as substance.

And this Love had a name: the Creator.

He was not merely loving. He was Love itself. Love in being, in doing, in dreaming. Love beyond logic, but not illogical. Love beyond reason, but never unreasonable. And in His domain, the Universal Kingdoms, this Love flourished not as a law imposed, but as a delight uncontained.

Every star danced to the rhythm of this Love. Every angel, every spirit-being, every glowing entity in the vast halls of Heaven pulsed with it. For Love was the gravity of the cosmos, the law not written on stone, but etched into the very structure of existence.

THE JOY OF THE FREE

Now it must be understood: the Creator could have made creatures who obeyed as wires obey electricity. But He did not.

He made them free.

He did not desire service driven by compulsion, but devotion born of wonder. It is a risky business, granting freedom, like handing matches to children in a library. But the Creator, in His fathomless goodness, considered the risk worth the love.

So He gave them the gift of will; a will that could choose joy...or reject it.

And Christian, the Co-Worker, stood by His Father from before time was born. Christian, the radiant expression of the Creator's own thoughts and being, through whom all things were made and by whom all things are sustained, shared the risk. For Love, when true, always does.

He was not simply an assistant in divine things, nor a servant carrying out errands. He was and is the visible form of the Invisible One. The face of Love that could be seen.

THE MUSIC OF THE KINGDOM

In those days (if one can speak of days in eternity), joy was the song of the Kingdom. It rang through every corridor of creation.

The angels never tired of their tasks. For in that realm, even work was worship. Every treaty between planetary worlds was not just a pact, but a poem; a celebration of peace written in gravity and song.

Loka, known then as the Day Star, was among the greatest of these beings. His light was second only to the Source. He danced upon the firmament, his voice calling forth harmonies that could make comets weep.

He was, by all appearances, incapable of betrayal.

But freedom—true freedom—has a curious property: it can

always be misused.

THE SOUND OF THE CROOKED SMILE

Sin came not like a storm, but like a tune. It whistled. It hummed. It chuckled. It knew all the chords to play.

"It's been a hard day's night," sang the darkness, with a grin too wide to be innocent. "And I've been working like a dog..."

The irony was breathtaking. Who had worked? Who had suffered? Not this imposter. Yet it sang as though it had been cheated of something. That is the strange logic of evil. It demands what it has not earned and resents what it once adored. Sin cannot create. It can only twist. Like a worm in an apple, it doesn't replace sweetness; it spoils it from within.

And the Creator? He did nothing. Not from weakness, nor indifference, but because Love never violates freedom, even when freedom flirts with destruction.

THE SMILE DARKENS

Loka stood on the edge of a choice. Not yet fallen. Not yet corrupted. But something had entered his thoughts: a question. A flicker of unease.

Why must we praise forever? Why must we always give? Why is Love always at the center?

These are not sins in themselves. In a world of freedom, even doubt has a place. But when questions turn to accusations, when curiosity curls into contempt, the descent begins.

The dark one, still unnamed, saw this and smiled. Not with joy, but calculation.

The infection had begun. Not with violence, but with envy masked as insight.

And so the perfect world began to tremble—not collapse, no, not yet—like a violin string caught between two notes.

THE FIRST TRAGEDY

There is no tragedy like a fall from beauty. The higher the height, the more terrible the tumble.

And yet even this, the Creator foresaw.

Even before the fall, the plan was written. Not as a reaction, but as a rescue prepared before the drowning began.

Love would not fail. It might be wounded. It might be mocked. It might even be nailed to a tree. But it would not, and could not, be defeated.

And so, the curtain falls for now. Not with a bang. Not even with a whimper. But with the fading echo of a song once sweet, now corrupted. A lullaby rewritten into a lie.

Yet even here, beneath shadow, a promise glows.

Because Love, as it turns out, writes the last chapter.

THE WATCHER

Sin Say stood at the edge of the light, watching the Kingdom pulse with breath and beauty. His form was undefined: slippery, shifting, smoke without flame. He sniffed the air, winced.

"Too clean," he muttered. "It smells like...hope."

A gust of warm wind coiled around him, and with it, a voice like thunder wrapped in silk.

"Trespassing, are we?"

Sin Say froze. Slowly, he turned.

There stood Syracuse. The dragon was massive, horned, and shimmering, his scales like starlight and molten iron. His seven eyes studied Sin Say not with suspicion, but with something worse: understanding.

THE DRAGON AND THE SHADOW

"Shadow-born," Syracuse said, voice calm but edged with humor, "you walk as though the ground should thank you for stepping on it."

Sin Say smirked. "And you sit as though the cosmos is your

front porch. What's next? A rocking chair and a 'Keep Off the Grass' sign?"

The dragon chuckled, thunder rolling in his chest. "If I posted a sign, you'd only steal the paint to scribble your own name."

"Ouch," Sin Say replied, pressing a smoky hand to his chest. "Accused of graffiti. What's next? Littering? Jaywalking?"

"Lies," Syracuse said smoothly, "though you prefer to call them...suggestions."

Sin Say wagged a finger. "Suggestions are polite lies. I elevate the art."

Syracuse leaned forward, scales glinting. "And yet smoke, no matter how you dress it, still disappears when the wind changes."

"Careful," Sin Say said with a crooked grin. "One gust and I might choke you first."

Syracuse laughed warmly, which somehow cut sharper than anger. "Choke me? You? Shadow, please. I've dined on comets. You're more like...seasoning."

Sin Say tilted his head. "Seasoning. I'll take that. Smoke gives flavor, after all. Without me, truth would taste bland."

"Strange," Syracuse replied, "I've never seen light complain that it needs help to shine."

Sin Say chuckled thinly. "You dragons are always so dramatic. Half your sentences never even finish, but everyone nods like you've solved existence."

"And you," Syracuse said, eyes narrowing in humor, "always finish your sentences and still manage to say nothing."

That landed. Sin Say forced a chuckle, gave a mock bow. "Bravo. The lizard wins this round."

"Dragon," Syracuse corrected, smiling.

Sin Say waved dismissively as he turned. "Titles, titles. You wear yours like a crown; I'll stick to my charm."

"Charm?" Syracuse said. "More like perfume. Strong at first, gone by morning."

Sin Say stiffened, but kept walking, muttering, "Who does that dragon think he is? Sitting there with all his shiny scales, like a walking jewelry shop. Thinks he knows me? Please. He don't know who he's messing with. We'll see. One day that lizard's going to trip over his own riddles."

And with a swirl of smoke and a smirk that didn't quite reach his eyes, the shadow moved on: outwardly unfazed, inwardly stung.

GRACE AND MERCY

Sin Say trudged on, muttering, until he heard sniffing. And...chirping?

Something broke the grass in tidy little patterns: mole-like tunnels weaving arcs around his feet. The ground puffed, and up popped a rainbow-furred creature with bright brown eyes.

"Hello, my brother!" it squeaked. "I'm Mercy."

Another popped up beside it, same eyes, same grin. "And I'm Grace!"

Together they chirped, "We show kindness to everyone we meet!"

Sin Say blinked. "You...what are you?"

"We're wombats!" they sang. "And also the postal service of the Kingdom!"

"Postal service?"

"Yes!" Grace chirped. "We deliver scrolls, letters, sometimes cookies."

"Snacks!" Mercy added proudly. "Though we eat about half."

Sin Say arched a smoky brow. "Do you even know who I am?"

Both shook their heads in perfect unison. "Nope!"

He chuckled darkly. "Clarence," he said. "My name is Clarence."

"Ooooh, very official," Grace whispered. "He probably wears gloves when he drinks tea."

Mercy gasped. "Do you?!"

"Of course," Sin Say lied.

The twins clapped their paws. "He's fancy!"

Before Sin Say could react, they shoved a scroll into his hand. "A message," Grace explained. "You looked like someone who needed one."

Sin Say unrolled it. The scroll was blank. He looked up, but the wombats had already vanished underground, giggles trailing behind them.

He stood alone, staring at the parchment. Blank. Empty. Yet somehow heavier than words. He hated it. Mostly because he didn't.

THE FISH ARMY

Smoke still curling around him, Sin Say drifted toward the River of Life. Its waters shimmered, ancient and alive. He bent to peer in, and the river rose. With a roar, it arched upward into a glassy wall, towering like the parted Red Sea. The ground trembled as the waters held. Fish leapt from the depths, sprouting legs, arms, armor. They formed ranks, shields flashing, spears raised. At their head stood a tall fish with a monocle, blue sash, and coral sabre.

"I am Captain D of the Fish Military," he barked. "State who you are and why you are here."

Sin Say bowed low. "Clarence. An angel from the Colossal City. Returning from a stroll."

Captain D squinted. "Suspicious. But polite." He tapped his monocle. "Permission granted."

The ranks parted. The waters folded back. A golden bridge rose from the depths, etched with ancient names.

Sin Say stepped onto it, forcing a smile. "Thank you, Captain."

The fish saluted in unison, tails slapping like drums.

As he crossed, he muttered, "Terrifying, really." Then softer, darker: "But every bridge leads somewhere. And some bridges...are meant to burn."

TOWARD THE GARDEN

Step by step, he moved toward the gates of the Colossal City, where the Edenic Garden gleamed. He could almost see Loka's radiance, could almost taste the envy rising like a feast prepared just for him.

Smoke trailed behind him. Shadows gathered at his heels. And Love, that immortal flame, flickered still in the distance, daring him to try.

THE BRIDGE

The bridge shone with a holy weight, gleaming with unseen words etched along its edge, old names, eternal promises. "Clarence" strolled across the bridge with a bounce in his step, humming a tune too chipper for the sacred silence. Something playful, almost childlike, twisted on his lips; a march fit for jesters, not angels. Every note was a mockery of the golden path beneath his feet.

CHAPTER FIVE

The Whisper and the Watcher

The morning light filtered through the branches in golden strands, like thoughts the Creator hadn't spoken yet. Loka, the Day Star, walked the Garden's quiet edges, his robes catching the breeze like sails unfurled on a cosmic sea.

There was peace here, but not stillness, of the kind that waits before a storm or the hush in creation's lungs when it senses change. Birds sang, though their trills were thinner than usual, as if even their throats held back. The River of Life sparkled nearby, its surface cutting diamonds from the sun, but beneath its beauty Loka felt a subtle weight pressing against the air.

He paused beside the Listening Tree. Its bark thrummed beneath his palm, a living drum keeping time with a heartbeat larger than his own. Leaves turned their silver undersides toward him as if to show their honesty. Far beyond the jeweled mountains ringing the Garden, something had shifted. He could feel it in his bones, like the press of weather before rain. It was not yet evil, not yet darkness. But it was...watching.

He let his hand fall. A smile flickered across his lips, though it did not reach his eyes.

"If you're watching," he murmured to the branches, "you'll need to do better than that."

The tree answered with a soft tremor. Wind, perhaps, or warning.

Each step carried him deeper into the winding paths of the Garden. Rare enough for such stillness. Rarer still for Loka to feel its weight pressing like a collar too tight.

Suspicion? Testing? Or, his chest lifted at the thought, perhaps honor? The ideas jostled each other like rival suitors. He adjusted his shoulders until the mantle lay just so. Radiance required posture.

A shadow flickered across the path. He turned sharply. Nothing. Only dew-jeweled grass and the soft dust his sandals had stirred. Yet the unease lingered, cool as water down the spine. He pressed on faster now.

"Day Star!"

The voice steadied him. Bruce approached with scroll-straight robes and clear, measuring eyes. The scholar always moved as if truth itself set his cadence.

"You walk quickly," Bruce said, falling into step.

"The morning urges it," Loka replied lightly.

"True." Bruce studied his face. "Yet haste is not the only thing in you."

"Do not mistake thought for trouble, old friend."

Before Bruce could answer, the underbrush gave a cheerful rustle, and Philo burst onto the path, wiping sap from his hands like a butcher proud of a clean cut. His grin could have lit a barn.

"Well now, look at us three, struttin' through paradise like roosters late for crowin'!"

"Not now, Philo," Bruce muttered, but Philo only winked.

"You can't tell me you ain't feelin' this hush," Philo said. "Garden's got that look, like a storm holdin' its breath. My bet? Change is comin'." He gave Loka a nudge. "Probably got your name scribbled all over it, Star-boy."

Loka's smile deepened; inside, something sharp turned. "Perhaps," he said. "Or perhaps correction."

Bruce frowned at the edge beneath his tone. Philo laughed. "Correction? You? That's like rebukin' the sun for shinin' too bright."

They walked beneath boughs that glittered like cut glass.

Honey-leaf and river-mist threaded the air. Distant music rose and fell, cleaving the morning into harmonies. Loka listened, but the music did not land the way it used to. Once it had opened him like a window; now it pressed from outside, and he could not decide whether to breathe deeper or hold his breath.

"Precedent is plain," Bruce went on, pointing with a finger that might as well have been a quill. "The Orion Accord established mutual recognition of gifts regardless of rank. Honor is granted for fruit, not for brightness."

Philo snorted. "Folks in Orion talk too pretty. Where I come from, you see a worker do the job, you hand him the shovel or the sword and get out the way. Fruit's good, but somebody's gotta swing."

Bruce kept his tone level. "Order is a melody, Philo; it cannot be shouted into tune."

"And melody don't clear a blocked river," Philo shot back. "You need hands."

"Hands without tune strike at random," Bruce said. "And random strikes the wrong thing."

"Unless the wrong thing's in the way," Philo grinned.

Loka let their argument wash past him. Their old debate—head and hand—usually amused him. Today, it rasped like fabric against a bruise.

Another flicker, this time between two seams of light where the canopy parted. Loka stopped so abruptly that Bruce checked his step.

"Did you see..." Loka began, then let it die. Bruce and Philo were already circling back through the Accord (precedent this, nuance that), oblivious to the prickling along his neck. He let them drift ahead and stood alone. The watcher was real. He could not prove it to another, but he knew it like he knew his own name. He lifted his chin and stepped into a band of sunlight that lay across the path like a testing-line.

"Come then," he said to the air, soft enough that only the

Listening Tree might overhear. "Let's see you in the open."

Only a moth obliged, swerving drunkenly through the gold, and then there: a distant, too-chipper hum. A childlike cadence, out of place in sacred quiet, as if someone were making light of holy things. It died when he turned his head.

"Ha!" a voice chimed near his elbow.

He nearly leapt as two rainbow-furred heads popped from a neat seam in the earth, perfectly symmetrical, perfectly delighted.

"Still sneakin' up on folks, I see," Loka said, shaking his head.

Mercy grinned. "Well, someone's got to keep you from walking faster than your peace."

"And we brought figs," Grace added, presenting a leaf bundle as if she were offering a treaty.

"For confidence."

Loka couldn't help himself. He smiled properly for the first time that morning. "Of course you did."

"We tried to smooth the morning out," Mercy said, lowering his voice, "but it wrinkled back."

Grace's nose twitched. "And something's watching. It doesn't know how to love yet."

"And it wants to learn the wrong way," Mercy added gravely.

They beamed at him once more, then vanished underground with a puff of soil. Loka stood alone again, figs warm in his hand, the warning colder in his chest. He moved on, slower. The path opened here, giving a view across the jeweled mountains and the living crystal boughs arching skyward. Music threaded the air like veins of light, angels' voices weaving harmonies that made the leaves answer.

His mind reached backward, unbidden, to another gathering. The memory rose so clean it might have been a song beginning again. Every seat filled, and Christian, the Co-Worker, standing at the heart like a pillar of morning. Loka remembered how the music had lifted then. How his own voice had threaded the lines, catching them, carrying them, delighting not in how high he could soar, but in how perfectly he could hold the chord. Joy had been simple then. Unthinking. Like water knowing how to be wet.

That was then.

Now the joy came with edges; the music required deciding. The thought troubled him and irked him for troubling him. Why should joy need guarding? Why should the Day Star measure joy at all?

A rustle to his left. He turned. Leaves settled as though a small thing had just slipped through. He caught again, faint and derisive, the echo of that jaunty hum. Playful notes in a sacred place. His jaw tightened.

Bruce and Philo waited where the path narrowed to a nave of trees, sunlight pooling in squares upon the ground.

"You lag, brother," Bruce said gently.

"I pace myself," Loka answered.

Philo leaned on a trunk, easy as a farmer on a fencepost. "Pace is good. But don't keep the choir waitin'. The song'll rise whether you're singin' or standin' off to the side."

Bruce tilted his head. "You heard it as well?"

"Heard what?" Philo asked.

"The hum," Bruce said simply. "Out of place. Childish."

Philo squinted at the trees. "I heard a squirrel with good lungs. If there's a child in these woods, it's a sneaky one."

Loka kept his face smooth. "Children don't mock."

"Some do," Philo said. "Then they grow up and get elected to committees."

"Philo," Bruce sighed.

"What? It's true."

They moved again, this time together. The path curved around a fountain whose spray formed letters that changed with the angle of light, spelling old names, older promises. Loka felt them touch him like hands. He wanted to shrug them off, then hated that he wanted that.

"You carry something," Bruce said quietly, so that only Loka could hear. "Lay it down before you go further. The Garden has a way of turning hidden weight into sound."

"My song is my own," Loka replied, smiling without warmth.

Bruce's eyes were kind and unyielding. "Your song is ours."

Philo clapped them both on the shoulders, breaking the moment. "Enough fuss. If there's glory to be handed out, I'm ready to clap; if there's correction, I'll stand behind you and look sympathetic."

"You could try standing in front," Loka said.

"I'm brave," Philo grinned. "Not foolish."

They reached a place where the light pooled thicker, the air drawn taut as if the Garden itself were holding its breath.

From somewhere behind the trees, light footsteps. Loka did not turn. He didn't need to. He could feel the gaze now like a thread tied at the back of his neck. He fixed his smile, evened his breath, took the last figs from his palm and set them on the fountain ledge.

"To the throne," he said.

"To the throne," Bruce echoed.

Philo tipped two fingers off his brow. "To the One who'll sort us out."

Loka straightened the mantle until it lay perfectly true. Every fold in place. Every beam precisely where it should be. He let the practiced smile return, bright as a new morning. Whatever awaited, he would not walk on as one uncertain. He would walk on as the Day Star, beloved and admired. The whispers could watch, the shadows could follow. But wherever the path bent...

He would shine.

CHAPTER SIX

The Day Star Descends

It did not begin with thunder. It began with silence.

Loka stood alone on the Watcher's Ridge, where the wind thinned and the stars blinked like distant memories. Below him stretched the Garden Realm in all its shimmer and song, with rivers like threads of firelight, mountains like jeweled towers, fields that moved in harmony with unseen breath. All of it shone beneath him, yet today it did not reach him. Not the harmony. Not the joy.

Only the hush.

He had always known the hush. It came before revelation. Before beauty. Before battle. It was the pause that framed everything weighty. But this hush was not the familiar expectancy of glory; it was different. Denser. Heavier. As though creation itself was holding back a confession it could not bear to speak. Loka felt it pressing at his chest, and he did not like the way it made him feel small.

What if the Creator was wrong?

The thought was not spoken aloud, yet it echoed in the hollow of his chest. Loka shivered not from cold, but from the way the thought curled inside him like smoke in glass. It did not belong there. It was foreign. And yet...it fit too easily.

He clenched his fists. "Not mine," he muttered. "Not my thought."

The stars overhead seemed to blink slower.

"Beautiful place, isn't it?" said a voice behind him.

The mocking hum from the Garden paths was gone. What replaced it was a voice smooth as polished stone, calm as still water.

Sin Say stepped from the shadows, clothed in soft gray light. His smile was kind. Too kind.

"I've always admired your post," he said, walking slowly toward the ridge. "It must be something, to live at the center of it all. The Creator's Day Star. His chosen."

Loka did not turn to face him. His eyes stayed on the horizon, on the far shimmer of the rivers, on anything but the figure approaching from behind.

"I didn't call for company," he said quietly.

Sin Say chuckled, a soft, almost fatherly sound. "Nor did I, but I sensed a soul in conflict. And I never miss such music."

There was no venom in his voice. No rage. Just familiarity, like an old friend offering counsel after a long journey.

"You've asked questions," Sin Say continued. "Good ones. Deep ones. Questions even Goodwin dares not speak aloud."

Loka's jaw tightened. "I do not question the Creator's wisdom."

"Oh, but you do," Sin Say said gently, stepping closer. "And that is not rebellion, Loka. It is awakening. Do you not see? You were made with brilliance. Made to lead. The others follow your voice without even thinking. And yet the Creator keeps you in chains of obedience, bound under banners of humility. Tell me. Why?"

Loka's throat ached. His lips parted, but no answer came.

Sin Say's eyes softened. "Go on. Say it out loud. The question you have carried."

The wind brushed Loka's face like fingers urging him forward. His heart pounded. He had thought it a whisper, a phantom murmur. But hearing it coaxed aloud, he could no longer deny it.

His voice cracked as he whispered: "Why not me?"

The words trembled in the air, and it was as though creation itself recoiled.

There it was.

The fracture. The smallest hairline crack in what had always been whole.

Sin Say smiled, not triumphantly but tenderly, like a physician coaxing truth from a reluctant patient. "You bear the light, Loka. You were crafted with beauty that rivals galaxies. Your song can split the air, heal wounds, stir armies. But they still look to the Creator. Still bow to Him. While you..." He let the silence hang, heavy and merciless. "...you remain a servant."

The word stung. Servant. Loka felt its weight now, heavier than mantle, heavier than crown. For all his brilliance, for all his radiance, he was still reflection, not source. The glass, not the fire.

Sin Say tilted his head. "Have you considered that perhaps the Creator fears what you could become if unbound?"

The hush deepened. Loka's breath came shorter. The thought sank like a hook. *Fears me?* It twisted something in him he had never named: the hunger not only to shine, but to be the sky itself.

LIBERTY'S VIGIL

High above the ridge, wings stretched wide, Liberty watched from the Perimeter. Her many eyes wept firelight. The scroll behind them turned of its own accord, letters shifting with sorrow. She had seen fractures before, but never in the Day Star.

The soundless cry rose in her chest: It has begun.

If she could have pierced the hush with a warning, she would have filled the heavens with her scream. But the order was clear: watch, record, wait. She bowed her head, feathers trembling, eyes burning like torches.

The ridge below seemed smaller than it should, as though the cosmos itself was leaning in.

THE DESCENT BEGINS

Loka turned at last. His eyes searched Sin Say's face for deceit, but found something worse: understanding. A mirror of his own unrest.

"Show me," Loka said, voice low, dangerous. "Show me what I've been denied."

Sin Say's smile deepened. Not cruel, not gloating, but sad. Almost reverent.

"I will," he said. "But once you see, you cannot unsee."

"I know," Loka whispered.

And the moment he did, the Garden shifted. The stars above dimmed. The wind grew sharp, as though the world itself recoiled. The hush cracked open into something hollow, echoing. The fields below shivered in dissonant chords. The River of Life seemed to hesitate in its flow, as if unwilling to move forward while its brightest servant faltered.

Liberty's wings caught firelight that was not fire. She pressed her brow against the scroll, whispering silent pleas no mortal tongue would ever know.

On the ridge, Loka took a breath, steadied himself, and stepped forward; off the ridge, off the path, and into the unknown. The ground beneath him did not collapse. The stars did not fall. The heavens did not roar.

It was quieter than all of that.

It was the sound of a fracture spreading through glass. The kind of break you cannot see until the whole pane gives way. And still, in his heart, Loka heard only one echo, steady and undeniable.

Why not me?

The echo did not fade when Loka left the ridge. It walked with him, step for step, through the hush between stars, a hairline crack running through glass that looked whole until the day it didn't. The Garden should have softened it. Instead, the air felt heavier, as if creation had bowed its head to listen. Leaves held their breath. The river hushed its laughter mid-ripple. Even the stones along the path seemed to settle their shoulders.

It was not silence; it was waiting. The kind that comes just before a messenger breaks the tree line with a word that can't be unsaid.

And beneath it all, steady as a drumbeat he could not unhear: *Why not me?*

CHAPTER SEVEN

A Meeting of Unequal Minds

Morning star-light sifted down through the ancient canopy, making the Garden shine as if every blade of grass had been polished for company. Near a pool shaped like a teardrop of glass, three figures stood in a half-circle: an intellectual, a wanderer, and the one they both called friend.

Bruce adjusted his cuffs with the dignity of a judge who ironed his robes with logic. "I'm telling you, he is not in the records."

Philo lounged against a fig tree, shaving curls off a twig with a knife that had seen more laughter than battle. "Maybe he ain't the record-keeping sort. Maybe he's just Clarence."

Bruce's look could have turned a comet around. "Clarence is not a designation used in four millennia of angelic registry. I checked twice. It isn't a name; it's a nursery rhyme."

Philo tipped the twig toward the pool. "Sounds like the sort who talks kinda sideways. Like he's got butter under his tongue."

Loka said nothing. He stood between them, calm as a quiet bell, studying the pool where a breeze had troubled the surface without touching their wings. When he finally spoke, his voice did not raise the dust.

"I met him at the edge of the forest," he said. "He claimed the Colossal City. Robe like a noble, eyes like someone who's watched too long."

Bruce's fingers tightened on the scroll under his arm. "Watched whom?"

"Me, I suppose. He asked too many questions and worked hard

to sound casual. His ease had edges."

Philo's knife paused. "That's the sort who asks where your garden is before he asks your name."

Bruce's tone sharpened. "Did he mention the Throne? Of the Son?"

Loka's head moved once. "Not once. He circled the fire for warmth but would not look into it."

Philo slipped the half-carved twig into his pocket. "That ain't poetry, friend; that's trouble."

For a moment, the Garden agreed. A bird that usually scolded the dawn swallowed its note. The pool settled into a perfect mirror and showed them three faces and, for a blink, a fourth. It was nothing more than a ripple, but Loka saw it. The fracture in him hummed. *Why not me?*

Bruce cleared his throat, as if to tidy the air. "Protocol requires we report any unregistered entity to the Inner Court immediately."

"And say what?" Loka asked gently. "A man with a half-smile came asking careful questions?"

"Exactly that," Bruce snapped, grateful for something exact. "Ambiguity breeds catastrophe."

Philo scratched his chin with the back of the knife. "Or we keep eyes open, ears to the wind, and don't run tell the choir every time a squirrel drops a nut."

Bruce stared. "You are comparing a possible infiltrator to a squirrel."

"Only if the squirrel's wearin' fancy robes," Philo said, easy as a porch swing.

A line almost like a smile touched Loka's mouth and left it. "For now, we wait. There's no war yet, just whispers. Let's not teach them to shout."

Bruce gave the smallest of grunts, the kind that meant, "I disagree but dislike shouting more than I dislike being wrong." He drew a breath to speak, then let it go unsaid. Philo flipped the knife once, caught it by the spine, and slid it away as if sheathing a joke.

They did not move at once. The Garden seemed to ask them not to. Wind came and went without rustling a leaf. Far off, the river tried a laugh and thought better of it. Loka glanced toward the low hills where dawn caught and held like light on a ring.

"Something shifts," he said, mostly to the air. "In the soil. In me. As if a truth is waiting to be told or twisted."

Bruce folded his arms, the scroll tight to his ribs. "Twisting implies a twister. Who benefits from this...this vagueness?"

Philo chuckled. "Folks who like to fish muddy water."

"Fishermen?" Bruce said, appalled by the metaphor.

"Metaphor's doin' the fishin', professor."

Loka let their rhythm run, the familiar friction of two good friends who sanded each other smooth. Their words were a tether; one of the few things he trusted not to fray in a wind. Beneath that trust, the hairline crack ticked along the pane.

Bruce took a step, then another, and the others fell in beside him, habit pulling them onto the sapphire-stone path that braided the orchard. Bees worked the fig blossoms like small monks at their prayers. Somewhere, a lily counted to three before deciding to open.

"Describe him precisely," Bruce said. "Height, bearing, diction."

"Taller than you, but not by much," Philo offered. "Diction like a stew: tasted good, but you couldn't name the spice."

Loka's answer was quieter and closer. "He wore his name like a borrowed robe: fine, but ill-fitted. And the sleeves hid his hands."

Bruce nodded, not because he understood but because the words made a shape he could chase. "Then we proceed by categories. He is an imposter, a rogue, or a poet, and we do not admit poets to security zones."

"World would be less interestin' if we did," Philo said.

"Less combustible," Bruce corrected.

They rounded a bend where the path pressed near the

orchard's edge. Between two trunks, the morning widened into a narrow window on the outer walks; nothing, really, but the sort of nothing that invites a pair of eyes. Loka's gaze caught there. A shadow seemed to lean, then stretched itself into simple shade, and the pane in him ticked again.

Bruce felt him pause. "What?"

"Nothing," Loka said, then, more honestly, "Something pretending to be nothing."

Philo lifted his hat to the shade and set it back down. "Well, if nothin' wants an introduction, it can step into the light. Otherwise, it can mind its manners."

"An entity that refuses to name itself," Bruce said, "often hopes you will do the naming for it. We must not."

Loka breathed in the Garden. It smelled of promise, old parchment, and the slight metallic tang that comes when stars are about to say something important. He could feel the speech forming—somewhere, with someone—and he knew it would arrive soon, not as thunder but as laughter. The thought made him uneasy and oddly comforted.

Philo nudged him, gentler than his boots suggested. "You're quiet in a way I don't like."

"I am thinking," Loka said.

"Thinking's good," Philo said. "So long as it doesn't build a fence."

Bruce agreed too quickly. "Quite right. Fences suggest property. Property suggests ownership. Ownership implies sovereignty. Sovereignty..."

"Belongs to the King," Loka finished for him, and the finishing steadied him a little.

They reached the teardrop pool again. Light lay across it like a blessing waiting for a forehead. Loka knelt, cupped water that weighed nothing and everything, and let it fall back through his fingers. The rings ran outward to the edges, kissed the moss, and returned; small waves coming home to report.

He listened.

Under the Garden's hum he heard the softest disturbance, like fur trying to be quiet and failing at it. It sounded like joy with bad timing. The corners of Loka's mouth remembered how to turn upward. He did not know why.

Bruce noticed. "What is it?"

"Nothing," Loka said, and for the first time that morning, the word "nothing" felt like a promise.

Philo squinted toward the far trees. "Feels like news is on the way. The good kind. Or the very loud kind dressed like the good kind."

"News," Bruce repeated, which was how Bruce said, "I will be ready before it arrives."

Loka rose. "We wait here."

"For what?" Bruce asked.

"For what is already coming," Loka said.

They stood together in an easy triangle; the kind forged by long miles and honest arguments. Above them, the branches made a cathedral roof of green and gold. Somewhere beyond, two small shapes tripped over roots and apologized to the roots; a song tried to harmonize with its own echo; a bell rehearsed the first note of a ring and then, shy, put it back.

On the far side of the orchard, where morning thinned into paths that knew how to keep secrets, a man lingered in the seam between shade and light. He wore the name Clarence like a festive mask and found that it fit. Behind the paper grin, an older name burned, one he tended like a coal. He had been on his way to the City to sulk properly, but the forest had a habit of giving him better ideas. And now the air itself promised guests. Invitations meant gatherings. Gatherings meant entrances. Entrances, if timed well, meant opportunity.

He smiled, all patience and teeth.

The Garden trembled so lightly that only those who listened with their souls could hear it.

And Loka, listening, heard it.

CHAPTER EIGHT

The High Invitation

The whispers hadn't stopped.

Not since the Garden itself began to lean into dawn as though expecting company.

Loka stood near the sapphire-stone path with Bruce and Philo, the pool of glass still rippling behind them. None of the three spoke, and the silence itself felt heavy until it was broken, not by thunder or trumpet, but by the sound of panting.

Two small shapes, Grace and Mercy, barreled out of the orchard like fuzzy comets gone off course.

"Mail call!" Grace wheezed, clutching a glowing scroll.

"Special delivery!" Mercy chimed, though he tripped on a root and nearly swallowed his scroll in the process. They landed in a heap of fur and scrolls and enthusiasm.

Bruce pressed his lips into a thin line. "Punctuality clearly wasn't in the job description."

Philo grinned widely. "Best mail service I ever saw. Half sermon, half circus."

Grace popped up, scroll in paw. "Correction: all circus, if you count the squirrels that followed us."

Mercy dusted himself off. "They were philosophical squirrels. Kept asking us about the meaning of acorns."

Bruce muttered, "Absurd."

"Profound," Mercy corrected.

Loka stooped and helped them gather the dropped scrolls. His fingers brushed one, warm, pulsing faintly like a heartbeat. His name glimmered across it in gold letters. The Garden's light seemed to bend toward it.

"The High Invitation," Grace announced solemnly. "Straight from the Hall of Lights."

Mercy nodded, chest puffed. "Signed by the King Himself. A celebration in honor of the Son."

The words sank like seeds into soil. Even Bruce's stiff shoulders eased. Philo's grin faltered into something closer to reverence. Loka's breath caught; for a moment he looked less like a leader and more like a child staring at a dawn he didn't earn.

Bruce adjusted his collar, regaining formality. "Then the meeting has not yet begun."

"Good," Philo said. "Hate showin' up after the snacks are gone."

Grace and Mercy handed out the scrolls, bowing so deeply they toppled into each other.

"Don't be late," Grace said, pointing at Bruce.

"And don't wear those boots," Mercy whispered to Philo. "The Hall of Lights has standards."

Philo puffed. "These boots are legendary."

"Legendary for scaring lilies," Mercy teased.

Bruce raised an eyebrow at Loka. "You will attend?"

Loka unrolled his scroll. The letters blazed for him alone: Feast at the Tree of Fellowship. His heart swelled and tightened all at once. Doubt crouched near the edges, but Bruce's hand on his shoulder was firm.

"Don't let shadows steal your seat at joy's table."

Philo slapped him on the back. "And put on your best robe. Might even wash my hat for this one."

The Garden itself brightened. The vines hummed like a choir tuning up. Even the river chuckled.

Grace and Mercy high-fived and darted off again, already humming a new song that rhymed invitation with salvation. They disappeared between the trees like laughter running ahead.

CLARENCE IN THE SHADOWS

Not far away, another figure had witnessed the exchange. Clarence, the mask over Sin Say's smolder, lingered at the orchard's edge. He had been sulking, rehearsing slights, but this? This was better. Invitations meant gathering. Gathering meant opportunity.

He slid from trunk to trunk, robe whispering. His eyes fixed on Loka's glowing scroll. His own hands were empty, but he would not stay that way.

"So," he murmured, lips curling, "a celebration for the Son. Perfect stage."

He lifted an imaginary goblet in mock salute. "Enjoy your laughter, little wombats. You've just told me everything I needed to know."

GETTING READY

What followed was a comedy the Garden hadn't seen in ages.

Bruce's dwelling shone with the glow of seven lamps, each angled precisely toward a mirror. He changed robes three times, debating shades of ivory only he could distinguish. He practiced introductions aloud. "Salutations, fellow scholars of the divine registry..." before coughing politely at himself.

"Less flourish," he whispered. "More gravity."

By contrast, Philo's cottage looked like joy had exploded inside it. Suspenders glowed faintly in the dark ("Safety and style," he assured a squirrel that stole one). His boots got a quick buffing with honey butter. He sang to himself in a voice that could have scared thunderclouds into rain.

"Lookin' sharp, Philo. Sharp enough to cut cheese at a feast."

And Loka? His preparation was silence. His room glowed with a single flame. He stood before a mirror, not to admire, but to honor the One who made him.

"I will praise You, for I am fearfully and wonderfully made," he whispered. His harp answered with a single note that sounded like morning breaking over water.

He bowed lower, eyes closed. "You formed me in Your light, and tonight I walk in that light. Keep me near Your heart. Keep me true when shadows rise."

Even Clarence made ready. In a chamber of his own shadows, he preened before a dark glass. Robe trimmed, hair set, eyes bright with mischief. "Why let them have the spotlight," he said softly, "when I can borrow it?"

THE KNOCK

Later that evening, Bruce and Philo arrived at Loka's elegant hillside abode. From its balcony one could see the Hall of Lights glowing below, alive with music.

"You knock," Bruce said.

"You're louder," Philo replied.

Philo banged on the door, then rang a crooked little bell he claimed was blessed by a prophet and a goat.

Inside, Loka's voice came, gentle and calm. "My brothers, I hear your footsteps like whispers on the wind. But tonight, I must meet you at the Hall."

"What?" Philo squawked. "You ain't comin' out?"

"The lilies wear perfume tonight. The stars lean low to see. And the moment...deserves an entrance."

Bruce rolled his eyes. "He's making a scene before the scene."

Philo chuckled. "Yup. That's our Loka."

They left, shaking their heads, leaving Loka to his chosen solitude. And beyond them, the Garden itself seemed to hum anticipation. Something more than a feast was gathering in the branches of time.

THE HALL OF LIGHTS

The Hall gleamed like a jewel under starlight, vines aglow,

crystalline walls alive with the laughter of dancing reflections. Angels, beasts, and creatures of otherworldly design mingled freely, sipping from cups that sparkled like the sea at sunrise.

Bruce and Philo entered just as the melody shifted. Fireflies spelled greetings overhead, but before they could interpret them...

"Well, well, well."

There he was.

Clarence.

His robe had too many buttons, and his grin had too many intentions. He leaned casually against a pillar shaped like an hourglass, as if he'd been waiting his whole life for this exact moment.

"Oh, stars," Bruce muttered, rubbing his temples. "I thought we had filters at the gate."

Philo laughed. "Aw, don't be like that, Brucey. He cleaned up nice! Look at all that shine. He's almost blinding."

"Like a chandelier that fell on its own ego."

Clarence, unbothered, stepped forward and extended a finger like one offering a precious gift.

"Gentlemen," he purred, "how radiant the night becomes when lesser minds gather near greatness."

Bruce narrowed his eyes. "And how fast that greatness becomes grating when it speaks."

"I love when you try to insult me with syllables," Clarence said. "It's like watching a turtle juggle. Admirable. Tragic. Ultimately pointless."

Philo choked on his drink.

Clarence adjusted his collar. "But really, I came for one reason."

He turned. He stilled. A hush fell over the Hall. The music softened. The light shifted. Even the lilies stopped swaying.

Something was happening.

THE ENTRANCE

He arrived.

Loka appeared not walking, but gliding inches above the marble-like floor. The jewels sewn into his mantle shimmered in impossible colors, not born of any earthly gemstone. Light itself bowed as it touched him, refracted and humbled.

He moved as music moves: effortlessly, inevitably, as if the stars themselves had parted to make way. His face carried both flame and tenderness. His hair shimmered like strands of midnight spun with lightning. His eyes held depths no artist could paint.

He was beautiful, not in the way of statues, but in the way of skies after storms.

All heads turned.

All mouths fell open.

Time held its breath.

Bruce blinked, voice low with wonder. "That's our beloved Loka…"

Philo nodded, a hand to his heart. "Heaven's Jewel."

Clarence gasped, but not with reverence. His eyes widened like one beholding a treasure too great to claim, too dangerous to leave untouched.

"There he is," he whispered, his smile curling. "My prize possession, my beloved son, soon to be the be-hated of all the world. And shall he not return the favor?"

He laughed, but only inside himself. And it was the kind of laugh that makes stars flicker for just a second.

A NOTE THAT BECOMES LIGHT

Loka's harp rested against his shoulder, strings shimmering like liquid fire under his touch. His voice rose with it: clear, full, and hauntingly beautiful. Each word carried weight, as though truth itself had borrowed his throat. Notes leapt into the air and did not fall; they lingered, heavy with glory, thick with light, as if creation itself was listening. The melody swelled beyond song; it became substance, like sound woven into the fabric of dawn. And as his voice climbed higher, reaching for a place words could not carry, the last note hung in the air, too strong to vanish, too alive to fade.

The final note of Loka's song—if it could still be called a note—was no longer sound alone.

It became substance.

A glowing spiral, like a golden staircase spun from song itself, unfurled in the air, coiling down gently from the place where time has no hold. The light it radiated was not earthly, not even heavenly as the angels knew it. It was origin-light, as if the very breath of the Creator had taken shape in a melody.

Loka, stunned, backed away. Even he did not know what was happening.

Colors unknown to mortal sight burst into existence like fireworks of truth and glory. The foundations of the Kingdom rumbled with anticipation. Light flashed so fiercely, so pure, that even the seraphim shielded their faces. The air trembled with the presence of something ancient, beautiful...and holy.

Then it happened.

A radiant figure stepped forth from the spiral walkway, walking not with haste but with royal exactness. His presence was like fire wrapped in mercy, and every particle of creation knew who He was.

The Son.

The Firstborn of all creation.

The One the scrolls had called by many names, but here...known simply and perfectly as Christian.

At His side, veiled but unmistakable, moved the Holy Advisor, a spirit of such deep wisdom and perfect stillness that His gaze alone stilled the sea of glass.

Then it came: a Voice, not from a mouth, but from the origin of all things.

A thunder from eternity itself:

"This is My Son, in whom I am well pleased."

The sound did not echo.

It stopped everything.

Every being from every galaxy, every planet, every rank and order of heaven's host fell silent.

Then they fell prostrate.

Even Bruce, who always had a line. Even Philo, whose knees hadn't touched ground in eons. Even Clarence, whose soul wrestled wildly within him, could not resist the call. He bowed. He confessed, with lips tight and heart torn, that Christian is Lord.

The vast Hall, the skies beyond, and the layers of light within light rang with worship too deep for words. And Loka, ever radiant, bowed lower than them all, his forehead touching the foundation stones of joy.

Only two remained standing.

The Son.

And the Advisor.

Together, they descended the spiral staircase of sound, each step illuminating more of what was to come.

And as they reached the ground...

CHAPTER NINE

Ripples Through the Kingdom

The heavens thundered with hallelujahs. Light poured like rivers down the golden slopes of eternity. Millions of angels lay prostrate, wings fanned out in reverent silence as the Son stood radiant, so glorious, even the stars stilled their spinning.

Clarence, too, was on his face. At least, that's what it looked like. His body pressed low, wings folded in perfect imitation. But inside, he was already standing. Watching. Measuring. Calculating. And moving. Like a shadow through a sunlit field, he slid between clusters of worshippers, slipping silently toward Loka. The Beloved knelt in awe, his face aglow from the lingering music of his harp. His heart was still split wide from wonder, still trembling from the Voice of the King.

That was the moment Clarence chose.

He leaned near Loka's ear, whispering softly enough to be mistaken for prayer.

"Strange timing, wouldn't you say? That your finest song should be swallowed whole. That you, Loka the Beloved, the Voice that stilled creation, should be so easily...overshadowed."

The words coiled, delicate, deadly.

But Clarence wasn't finished. He lingered, lips curved like a serpent ready to strike again.

"Enough." Bruce's voice cut through the incense-heavy air. He stood a short distance away, arms crossed, eyes sharp as lightning. Philo loomed beside him, his posture far more relaxed but his gaze just as fixed.

Clarence straightened slowly, the picture of innocence.

"Brothers," he purred. "Surely you misheard. I was only encouraging him."

Bruce's jaw clenched. "You were planting seeds. I've heard that tone before. I've heard it in you."

Philo scratched his chin. "Can't say I like it either. Private whispers in the Hall of Lights? That's shady business, even for you, Clarence."

Clarence placed a hand on his chest in mock offense. "Shady? In the presence of the Son Himself? Gentlemen, your paranoia dishonors the very throne we stand before."

Bruce stepped closer, lowering his voice. "You're clever with words. Too clever. You twist them into traps. Loka doesn't need your riddles."

Clarence's smile thinned. "And you think he needs your chains? You don't see him, not truly. He carries a depth you cannot fathom. The King may overlook it. You may scorn it. But I...I honor it."

Philo snorted. "Honor? Sounds more like you're feeding him poison and calling it perfume."

The three locked eyes: Bruce rigid with suspicion, Philo braced like a shield, Clarence a snake coiled but unstruck.

In the tension, Loka rose slowly. His face still glowed with awe, but now a shadow flickered beneath his eyes. He looked at Bruce. At Philo. At Clarence. Then, without a word, he turned and walked away.

"Loka..." Bruce began, but Philo held up a hand.

"Let him go."

And so he went, past fountains that once sang with his harp, past vines that whispered scripture, past gardens where stars bloomed in quiet praise. He did not look back.

Clarence followed like smoke on the wind, his grin sly. But this time he wasn't alone. A shadow shifted, massive and scaled, blocking his path.

Syracuse.

The great dragon leaned against a tree that had never been planted, his wings folded like resting mountains. One eye was open, the other shut, as always. His teeth flashed in a grin too wide to be safe.

"Well, well," Syracuse drawled. "If it isn't the serpent trying to slither where light still lingers."

Clarence stiffened. "Stand aside, old beast. You're out of your depth."

Syracuse yawned, smoke curling lazily from his nostrils. "Depth? Clarence, my boy, I nap in depths that would drown your schemes. Why not try honesty for once? It'd fit you like an ill-tailored robe."

Clarence's eyes narrowed. "You mock what you don't understand."

"Mock?" Syracuse chuckled. "No, no, I laugh because if I don't, I'd cry. And my tears flood valleys." He leaned closer, lowering his voice. "The King sees you, Clarence. And worse for you, so do I."

Clarence hissed, the honey gone from his tone. "Stay out of my way, dragon. Or I'll split that grin from snout to scale."

Syracuse's grin only widened. "Try it. Just know when I roar, even lions listen."

For a moment the air thickened—scales against sneer, wisdom against venom—then Clarence slipped away like smoke before a storm, muttering curses under his breath.

At last, Loka reached the cliff, a vast edge of starlight overlooking the unshaped void. The emptiness stretched out, vast and honest, a beauty untouched by decree or comparison.

Why was I made to shine...only to be overshadowed?

The ache gnawed deeper.

Clarence appeared beside him once more, no longer hiding, no longer pretending. His voice slithered into the silence.

"Because even light can be hidden beneath the right weight."

The words pressed like a stone on Loka's chest. He closed his eyes. The memory of the Son's glory still blazed, but Clarence's whisper wound through it like smoke through sunlight. The questions multiplied. The ache spread.

"Who am I if not chosen?" Loka whispered.

Clarence leaned closer, his eyes glinting. "You are more than chosen. You are mine."

The silence stretched. The universe seemed to lean in. Every star, every wing, every throne waited, trembling.

And then it came: not a song, not a prayer, but a word that split eternity in two.

"Father."

The name left Loka's lips like a wound torn open. Not to the King. Not to the Creator. But to Sin Say.

The veil ripped. Across the Kingdom, light screamed. The skies shuddered. The river of glass fractured with a sound like the breaking of time. Galaxies reeled. Thrones shook. Angels fell from their stations in horror. Even the stars themselves dimmed, as if they had covered their faces in grief.

And then came the cry.

Liberty.

Her screech tore through the cosmos, a sound that was not mere noise but judgment itself. It pierced mountains, rattled stars, shook the roots of Eden and the heights of the heavens. Every eye she bore flared with fire. Her voice was a trumpet of truth, shrieking against the lie that had just been spoken.

The four lions answered.

From the corners of the Kingdom, their roars rose, weaving together into a thunder that split time's fabric. Their voices shook the very perimeter of creation, a declaration that justice still stood guard though the Beloved had fallen.

In the Hall of Lights, Bruce collapsed, clutching his chest as if struck. Philo staggered, his steady frame rocked like a tree in a storm. Every being knew, without messenger, without decree, that something had been broken that would never be undone.

And at the cliff of starlight, Loka lowered his head, no longer Beloved.

A star had fallen.

But when the roar of justice faded and the screech of Liberty no longer split the skies, silence pressed in. Not peace, but aftermath. The kind of silence that leaves the soul stripped bare.

Loka drifted from the cliff's edge, wings heavy, steps unsteady. The Garden no longer called to him, not the way it once did. Its songs felt distant, its fragrance foreign. Rest would not come, not here, not now.

So he walked. Past familiar fountains, past paths once lined with praise, until the way narrowed into a realm few dared to tread. A place unadorned, unperformed, unafraid to show him to himself.

The Hollow Places waited.

CHAPTER TEN

The Shadow of the Hollow Places

It was not night, but it felt like it. Loka moved quietly, his robes dimmed by distance and dust. Behind him, the songs of the city still echoed faintly, like the memory of a dream slipping through half-sleep. Every note seemed farther away, less certain.

Before him stretched the Hollow Places, a realm not forbidden, but rarely visited. Not because it was dangerous, but because it was...honest. The ground was soft with silence, almost spongy beneath his steps. Trees stood like ancient watchers, their bark veined with faint lines of light that pulsed as though breathing. No wind stirred their branches. No birds dared to sing. The air was neither warm nor cold but carried a weight that pressed on the soul more than the skin.

This was not a place for performance. It simply existed: bare, unbothered, unmoved.

Loka sank beneath a tree that wept light from its limbs. The branches shimmered, threads of silver dripping toward the ground, yet vanishing just before they touched. He pressed his hand into the soil and felt it, cool, still, honest.

The words slipped from him before he could catch them. "I feel like I'm being peeled. Like my armor is dissolving, one truth at a time."

A voice answered, not from the tree, but from the quiet itself.

"That is what the Hollow Places do. They remove what you do not need."

Loka startled, then turned. The Holy Advisor stood nearby. Not intruding, only available. His presence was like standing near a still pond: it pulled the eye, calmed the heart, yet hinted that its depths went on forever.

"I didn't summon you," Loka said softly.

"You didn't have to."

There was no judgment in the Advisor's tone. Only invitation.

"You've come far," he continued. "And you've begun to ask questions. Real ones."

Loka's gaze dropped to the earth. He traced a line in the soil with his finger. "They say questions are dangerous."

"Only to lies."

The Advisor lowered himself gracefully, robes folding untouched by the dust. Sitting beside Loka, he looked not like a distant teacher but a companion willing to walk the same road.

"You are not wrong to pause, to ache, to wonder," he said. "What matters is where those questions take you. And who walks with you while you ask them."

Loka exhaled, long and heavy. It rattled in his chest before slipping free. "I didn't mean to doubt."

"You didn't," the Advisor replied. "You meant to understand. That is very different."

The silence that followed was not empty. It was alive, steady, like a heartbeat too great to be rushed. The Hollow Places carried it well. Then, with a quiet motion, the Advisor lifted his hand. Space itself unfolded like fabric, parting to reveal a window of light.

"There is something you must see."

Through it, Loka beheld a world unborn, still wrapped in the Creator's intent. Oceans shimmered like liquid glass. Mountains stretched high as if waiting for songs to crown them. Stars hung suspended like seeds before planting.

Then, a garden, vast, lush, fragrant with possibility. Every leaf seemed tuned to a melody not yet sung. In its center stood two figures. Human, but more. Sculpted by love. Breathed into being.

Loka leaned closer, breath held. "What are they?"

"Your future family," the Advisor whispered. "Children of dust and glory. They will walk the very ground you now glimpse."

Loka watched as the man stirred awake. His eyes opened wide with wonder, hands trembling as they touched creation for the first time.

Then came the woman, not shaped from clay, but drawn from closeness. Not placed beside the man as a stranger, but brought from him, bone of bone, breath of breath.

The man's eyes shone with astonishment. With a voice trembling between laughter and awe, he spoke, "You...are mine. Not as possession, but as poem. You are the answer to a question I didn't know I'd asked. When I look at you, I see the shape of joy."

Loka's own breath caught, chest tightening as though something long-forgotten had stirred within him.

The scene faded. The window closed.

"They will inherit the struggle," the Advisor said. "But also the song."

"Why show me this?" Loka asked, still leaning forward as though the vision might return if he willed it.

"Because you are part of the song. And the enemy has begun to rewrite your melody."

Loka's eyes flickered. A name trembled on his lips.

"Clarence."

The Advisor's gaze hardened, though his voice remained steady. "He speaks half-truths dipped in honey. He tempts not with pain, but with pity."

Loka rose slowly, brushing the silver dust from his robes. His wings shifted uneasily at his back.

"I need time."

"You have it," the Advisor said. "But remember, time is a canvas. Use it well."

And with that, he vanished, like a candle snuffed by unseen wind.

Loka stood alone once more. But the silence of the Hollow Places had changed. It no longer rang hollow. It pressed gently, like a question waiting for an answer. He looked up at the sky, though he was unsure what the stars saw in him now. All he knew was this: the story was not yet over.

Not for him.

Not for anyone.

CHAPTER ELEVEN

When the Garden Held Its Breath

Bruce had worn a path into the grass beside the Edenvines, a precise little corridor of flattened green that measured, by Philo's estimation, exactly the length of a stubborn thought. He paced it like a metronome set to "worry," hands clasped behind his back, jaw working on words he refused to say aloud.

Philo had found a sun-warmed stone and claimed it like a throne. He'd started whittling a twig with a knife so dull it might have been a spoon in disguise. The shavings came off in dignified sighs, more tired than neat.

"Been waitin' so long," Philo said, flicking a curl of wood and missing the river by a scandalous margin, "my heart-whiskers are startin' to tingle."

"You do not have heart-whiskers," Bruce replied without looking up.

"I do," Philo insisted mildly. "They sprout in times of discernment. Very sensitive instruments. Detect comin's, goin's, and general foolishness."

"Then shave them," Bruce said. "They're picking up a storm."

The Garden had not dimmed, not quite, but its brightness had gone thoughtful. The lilies sang softer, as if saving their voices. The river, which was usually pleased with its own music, hummed one low note and held it. Even the Edenvines, those faithful green cathedrals, trembled without wind, leaves touching leaves like hands in prayer.

Philo lowered the knife. "I know what you're gonna say."

"I doubt it," Bruce murmured.

"You're gonna say the harmonies are thin and the lilies are off-key." Philo sniffed the air.

"And you're right. The place sounds like a choir that lost its bass."

Bruce stopped pacing and finally turned. "Do you feel it too?"

"Yeah." Philo's grin slipped. "I been jokin' at it, but I feel it. The kind of quiet that ain't peace, just a hush that's gettin' heavy."

Bruce rubbed his temple with two fingers, his habit when words lined up and refused to march. "He has been gone longer than he should. Loka does not vanish. He withdraws, yes, but he leaves a note in the air. This," he gestured toward the listening trees. "this is not withdrawal. This is absence."

Philo rolled the twig between his palms. "You think he wandered back to the Hollow Places?"

"Possibly." Bruce resumed his measured corridor. "He went to be stripped of noise. To be honest. But honesty is not always gentle." He glanced at the silver arches. "And there are voices that love an emptied room."

"Say his name," Philo said, the humor gone from his tone.

Bruce hesitated, then let the word fall like a pebble that knows it is heavier than it looks. "Clarence."

Philo's mouth tightened. "That slick-tongued chandelier."

"A chandelier?"

"Pretty to look at, dangerous if it falls on you, and always tryin' to be the brightest thing in the room." Philo snorted. "He's slipperier'n a greased eel wearin' silk socks. Never walks straight. Comes in at an angle, like a lie lookin' for a polite place to sit."

"Poison in perfume," Bruce said.

"That's him," Philo agreed. "Got a way of sayin' things so your heart nods before your head wakes up. And when your head does wake, you already swallowed the seed."

Bruce's mouth threatened a smile and failed. "You are not wrong."

Philo stabbed the twig into the dirt and left it there quivering like a tiny, indignant flag. "Next time we see him, he's gettin' a piece of my mind. Not a crumb. A slice."

"Are you certain you can spare it?"

"Ha." Philo wagged a finger. "Joke while you can, scholar. When I tell that fox what I think, I'll use all the big words you love so much. I'll string 'em like lanterns and throw the whole rope at him."

Bruce actually smiled briefly, like a candle catching and then remembering itself. "You will throw lanterns."

"I will," Philo said. "And if that don't work, I'll use my boots."

The river purred in their direction, disapproving as only a river can. Philo lifted his hands in surrender. "Kiddin'. Mostly."

They fell quiet again. A leaf tumbled from an Edenvine and did not touch ground, evaporating instead into a curl of light. Bruce watched it fade, eyes narrowing.

"He is vulnerable to admiration," Bruce said at last.

"Loka?"

"Yes. He receives praise like rain. Most gardens drink and grow. But praise can flood, and floods carry things away."

Philo nodded slowly. "Clarence knows that. He don't shove. He drips. Drip, drip, drip, then suddenly you're standin' in a river you didn't know you stepped into."

"True." Bruce paused. "He will not announce malice. He will announce concern. 'Are you overlooked, Loka? Are you under-honored? Are you eclipsed?' He will say the word 'justice' until it no longer means the King's will."

Philo whistled softly. "You just wrote his script."

"It is an old script," Bruce said, voice low. "He merely performs it with better staging."

Philo scratched his chin. "You ever notice how he smiles with no warmth? Like a lamp givin' off light but no heat. That ain't natural. Light's supposed to warm what it touches."

"Mm." Bruce looked back to the arches. "When we see him, we

speak plainly."

"That's what I've been sayin'," Philo replied. "I'll do the plain, you do the speak. 'Clarence,' I'll say, 'you're slicker'n ice on glass and twice as useless. Quit whisperin' around our brother.' And if he grins that grin—oh, I know that grin—I'll say, 'Wipe it off before I help you.'"

Bruce exhaled, a sound too tired to be a laugh and too fond to be a sigh. "Do not help him."

"No promises." Philo's eyes softened. "Truth is, I'm scared for Loka."

"As am I."

Philo looked at his hands, big and capable and suddenly unsure. "What do we do when the person who pulls us into praise starts sinkin' in a song we can't hear?"

"We stand where he will return," Bruce said. "We make a place for him. We hold the line of what is true so he has a line to catch."

"And if he don't reach?"

"Then we keep holding," Bruce said, and it sounded like both a prayer and a punishment. "We wait. Faith has a patience that compels the impatient to loathe it."

Philo winced. "That was definitely a Bruce sentence."

"Thank you."

"Not a compliment."

They let the silence stretch until it became almost comfortable again, like a cloak that had found the right shoulders. Overhead, a skein of birds crossed, then dissolved, choosing stillness instead of flight. A squirrel peered from an Edenvine, decided the moment was above his pay grade, and retreated.

"Remember when we first met him?" Philo asked suddenly. "He was all glow and laughter, but his eyes were old. Not tired, just...full. Like he'd seen more sunrises than the sky could count, and loved each one on purpose."

"I remember," Bruce said. "He asked me a question about a psalm I had not yet memorized, and then answered it with a song that made my argument irrelevant."

"He asked me if my boots squeaked because they were shy," Philo said. "Then he made 'em sing. You ever heard leather sing? I have."

"Frequently," Bruce said. "Against my will."

Philo's grin returned, faint and faithful. "He'll come back," he said, as if saying it could help make it so.

Bruce did not answer.

A hush fell again, different this time. Not the ache of absence, but the tight, thin silence of something squeezing through the seams of the world. The Edenvines lifted their leaves as one. The lilies stopped singing altogether, which they almost never did. The river drew its note down to a thread.

Philo stood, knife forgotten on the stone. "You feel that?"

Bruce's head tilted, listening with more than ears. "Yes." He swallowed. "Yes."

Philo's voice fell to a whisper. "Is it him?"

Bruce did not trust his voice. He only nodded.

From the silver arches at the Garden's fringe, a shape formed as if the light itself were remembering how to be a body. Robe first, dark at the edges, like morning that had decided not to chase the night. Then, wings folded too close, as if they had learned fear.

Then, face, beautiful, always beautiful, but carrying a gravity that had not belonged to him before.

Philo's hands opened and closed without instructions from his mind. "Hey there, brother," he breathed, though Loka had not yet stepped fully through.

Bruce's heart struck his ribs hard enough to be counted. He felt words gallop to his throat and stop like horses at a cliff.

One step, then another. Loka crossed the threshold. The Garden did not brighten. It did not dim. It simply held its breath so completely that all the world was a held note, waiting for whatever would strike it next.

Bruce and Philo did not move. Neither did the leaves. Loka

stood among them, wings tight, eyes unreadable, light cupped in his features like a memory that didn't know whether to stay or run.

And the chapter ended the way some prayers do: not with an answer, but with an arrival.

CHAPTER TWELVE

The Turning Point

The Garden did not welcome them. Its vines shivered as if touched by frost. The lilies curled inward, their petals tight against the night. Even the river, faithful in its song, hushed to a whisper too faint to carry. Creation itself seemed to know what was coming and dared not rejoice.

Bruce and Philo paced near the edge of the clearing, each step heavier than the last. They had been waiting, searching the horizon for any sign of their brother.

Then the air shifted. From the silver arches came two figures: one radiant, though dimmed; the other radiant only in appearance.

"Brother," Philo whispered, his voice catching before the word finished.

Loka stepped forward, wings drawn tight, his face as unreadable as clouded glass. Clarence walked just behind, hands clasped, lips curled in that half-smile that always looked like it was hiding something.

Bruce's eyes sharpened at once. "Of course," he muttered.

Philo spat the twig from his teeth. "Knew we'd see him slitherin' around. Slicker'n grease on glass."

Clarence only smiled wider. "Now, now. No need for suspicion. I merely found our friend here wandering the outer edges. Imagine my delight in returning him safely."

Bruce folded his arms, voice like flint. "Safe is not the word I'd use."

Philo stepped closer, his boots heavy on the grass. "You always show up when shadows get thick, Clarence. Always whisperin', always smilin', never sayin' straight what you mean. I don't trust anyone who shines without heat."

Clarence bowed slightly, mock-polite. "And yet here I am. Perhaps the King Himself saw fit to send me."

Bruce snapped, "The King has never needed your errands."

The air tightened. Loka stood between them, silent. His eyes darted once toward Bruce, then toward Philo, then back to Clarence, who placed a hand near his shoulder as if claiming him by proximity alone.

Philo's voice broke the stillness. "Loka, brother, you hearin' this? This fox is poison dressed in perfume. He don't mean you no good. Don't let him plant them seeds in your soil."

Clarence laughed softly. "Seeds? My dear Philo, I don't plant weeds. I water what's already there. Doubts. Questions. Honest longings the rest of you would rather shackle than face."

Bruce's eyes burned. "You twist truth like vines around a dead branch. You dress pride in pity and call it compassion."

Clarence turned to him smoothly. "And you chain brilliance in bureaucracy, Bruce. You and your endless scrolls, your measured judgments. Have you ever truly seen him? Truly honored him? Or have you feared what his light might outshine in you?"

Bruce faltered for half a breath, but Philo cut in, his fists clenched. "Don't you turn this on us. He's our brother. Our friend. We'd bleed before we let him fall."

"Fall?" Clarence's tone sharpened. "Is that what you call rising above chains? You envy him. You envy his song, his radiance, his place. I honor it. I tell him what he already knows but fears to say: that he was born to lead, not follow. Born to be more than just another voice in someone else's choir."

Bruce stepped forward, trembling with anger. "Born to worship, not to usurp. The crown belongs to the Son. Always has. Always will."

For the first time, Loka stirred. His voice was low, strained. "Enough."

They all turned. His face was troubled, beautiful still, but lined with a sorrow that looked older than time itself.

Bruce softened instantly. "Brother, listen to me. You are not lost. Whatever Clarence has whispered, whatever shadows press on you, you still belong. You still have a place in the light."

Philo's voice cracked, pleading. "Don't do this, Loka. Not like this. Please. You was made for glory, not for graspin'. For singin', not schemin'. Don't throw away what's still yours."

THE GARDEN'S SUSPICION

For the first time, Clarence's smile faltered. His eyes sharpened, the warmth in them peeling away like paint from old stone.

Bruce stiffened. "You're circling words again. Always with riddles, never with truth."

Philo jabbed a finger toward him, jaw tight. "I knew it. We knew it all along. Somethin' about you ain't right. Slicker'n a snake in tall grass."

Clarence only tilted his head, lips curling back into that half-smile that never reached his eyes. "And yet, here I stand. Beside him, when the rest of you only stand in the way."

Bruce's voice trembled with anger. "Poison dressed as friendship."

Philo growled, fists clenching. "He don't need your kind of loyalty."

But Clarence didn't argue. He didn't defend. He simply laid a hand near Loka's shoulder, his smile returning like a mask. "Strange, isn't it, how suspicion always speaks loudest when fear is near?"

Loka flinched, torn in two. His silence stretched like a shadow, and the Garden seemed to lean closer, waiting. And then, without another word, he turned. Wings pressed tight, face unreadable. He walked with Clarence into the waiting dark.

The vines shivered. The lilies curled. The river hushed. Creation sighed; the river held its breath. Creation itself leaned in. And then Loka spoke.

His words came halting, trembling, breaking under their own weight. "I want...to do what is right." His voice faltered. "But I can't. It's too late. My place...is already lost."

The silence afterward was unbearable.

Bruce staggered, clutching his chest as if struck. "No..." he whispered. "No, not like this."

Philo wept openly, fists pressed to his eyes. "Brother, please..."

But Loka did not meet their eyes. He turned slowly, wings folding tighter against his back as though trying to hide their fading light.

Clarence placed a hand on his shoulder, triumphant. "There now. You've chosen. And soon, all the worlds will see what you were meant to be."

Together, they stepped into the shadow.

The Garden did not brighten. It did not dim. It sighed a long, low sound that carried through every root, every leaf, every star above. The sigh of innocence breaking.

And Bruce and Philo stood frozen, their hearts torn wide, as the brother they loved disappeared into the dark.

CHAPTER THIRTEEN

Seeds in the Dark

The shadows swallowed them whole. The further they walked from the Garden, the fewer stars dared to shine. Even the wind grew cautious, brushing past their wings like a servant afraid to speak. Behind them, the Garden held its breath. Ahead of them, the silence thickened. And in that silence, Clarence found his stage.

Loka walked with his wings folded so tight they ached. He did not speak. He did not lift his eyes. His light, once a song in itself, flickered like a candle at the mercy of its own wax. Clarence matched his pace with elegant patience, every step measured, every breath deliberate. His smile did not fade; it deepened, as though the darkness itself had become his audience. He let the silence ripen until it threatened to snap. Only then did he break it, voice soft as velvet, heavy as stone.

"Do you feel it, brother? The surrounding hush? Creation itself pausing...waiting. Not with fear. With awe. The universe senses what you are becoming."

He slowed his stride, tilting his head to study Loka in the dim light. His words lingered in the air like incense, coiling, clinging.

"You walk as one wounded, but wounds do not diminish gold. They reveal the shine beneath the dust. Tell me," his voice caressed the pause, "do you not wonder why every vine recoils when you pass, every stream stills its song? They recognize a king in the making."

Loka's jaw trembled. He wanted to answer but found no strength. At last he muttered, voice low and broken. "I don't want...their silence. I only wanted my place back."

Clarence's smile curved like a blade. He slowed, pivoting just enough to catch Loka's downcast eyes.

"Your place? Back?" He let the word dangle, sharp as glass. "What weak language, Loka. Back is for servants retreating to their posts. Back is for those content to carry another's crown. No, no, no, your place is not behind. It is before. Always before."

The echo of his words seemed to walk ahead of them. Loka's steps faltered ever so slightly. The shadows leaned closer, listening.

Clarence's tone dipped lower, almost intimate. "They speak of worship, but you were made to be more than chorus. Your voice bends the heavens. Your brilliance does not bow; it commands. Why do you think Bruce trembles, or why Philo pleads? Not because they doubt you, but because they fear you. Fear that you will realize what they have always known," he whispered as though unveiling a secret forged in fire, "that you outshine them all."

Loka's breath caught. A flickering memory of the Garden, of lilies curling and vines recoiling, of Bruce's tears and Philo's cracked voice, stabbed his chest. For a heartbeat, he almost turned. Almost.

But Clarence saw it. He saw the hesitation, and like a seasoned actor, he filled the silence before it could become strength.

"Do not mistake their begging for love. Love does not bind. Love does not whimper at your feet, afraid you will walk away. No, brother, what they call love is fear draped in sentiment. They fear losing you because they cannot imagine themselves without you. That is not love. That is prison."

The word prison struck the air like iron. Loka flinched, wings twitching at his back.

Clarence straightened, his shadow stretching long and tall as though crowned by the darkness itself. His voice gathered strength, each phrase cut with authority.

"The Son wears His crown as though none else could ever deserve it. And yet, your light rivals His. Does He thank you for it? No. He tucks you beneath His radiance, like a master hiding the brilliance of his servant lest it outshine His own. And you," he jabbed a finger softly against Loka's chest, "you ache under it, though you dare not name the ache. I name it for you: buried greatness."

Loka staggered half a step, his hand instinctively brushing the place Clarence had touched, as though the words themselves had weight. His lips parted.

"I...I only ever wanted to be faithful."

Clarence's laugh was not loud. It was worse: quiet, sharp, dismissive.

"Faithful? Faithfulness is the song of the content. You were not born for contentment. You were born for wonder. For brilliance. For worship that does not rise upward only, but flows outward from you to others. To lead. To rule."

He let the word rule hang in the night like forbidden fruit glinting in the moonlight. The air itself seemed to lean closer. A star above them dimmed, as if ashamed.

Loka's silence screamed louder than any word. His chest tightened. Part of him wanted to shout Bruce's name, or remember the laughter of Philo when the world was still innocent. But the other part, the part wounded, hungry, restless, leaned closer to Clarence's flame.

And Clarence knew it.

"Do you not see? This ache is not curse, it is calling. Why else would creation itself hush when you pass? Why else would the Garden grieve, if not because it knows its keeper has outgrown it? You are not merely angel, Loka. You are destiny dressed in flesh of light. They tremble because they glimpse what you could be, if only you dared."

He circled Loka slowly, predator and poet in one. His wings brushed the air like whispers, his eyes gleaming with fire.

"And I tell you this, not as flatterer, not as foe, but as the only one who dares speak what heaven hides: you were not born to follow. You were born to be followed."

Loka shuddered. His wings pressed tighter, as though holding himself together. His voice cracked.

"If I turn fully...there is no going back."

Clarence's grin widened, triumph flickering in his gaze.

"There never was a back. Only forward. Only higher. Only what waits when you stop bowing to chains." He lifted his hand, palm up, as though offering a throne carved of air. "Walk with me, and you will see how small their crowns are. Walk with me, and we will awaken others who are waiting, aching as you ache, bound as you are bound. Together we will tear down the walls they call 'order' and raise a new kingdom from the ruins."

Loka's eyes fell shut. In the darkness behind them, he saw Bruce's tears, Philo's fists pressed to his face. He heard the river's hushed song, the Garden's sigh. He felt the weight of innocence slipping.

But he did not speak. Silence became his answer. And Clarence received it with a bow, as though silence itself were worship. They walked deeper into the dark.

Above them, another star flickered and dimmed, as though ashamed to watch. The Garden did not weep; it unraveled, one petal, one leaf, one trembling star at a time.

CHAPTER FOURTEEN

The Slight and the Serpent

The hush did not rush them; it received them. It rose like an ancient archway, trees bending inward until their branches stitched a vaulted canopy above. The air itself seemed painted in shadow, thick and still, as though some unseen hand had brushed silence across the scene. Ahead, the path thinned into the distance, vanishing where the dark swallowed all horizons.

No stars intruded. No wind stirred. The silence lingered, not empty but alive, like a gallery of shadows holding its breath.

Here, in that painted stillness, Loka walked. His wings remained folded so tight they ached, every step heavier than the last. His light, once a song in itself, flickered faintly, like a flame fighting its own wax.

Clarence moved beside him with the grace of an actor who already knew the ending. Every stride measured, every breath deliberate, his smile curving deeper as though the silence itself had become his audience. He let the hush stretch until it threatened to snap. Only then did he speak, his voice low and almost reverent, as if he, too, were afraid to disturb what he meant to break.

"Glory has a way of choosing an audience," he murmured. "And a way of choosing a thief."

Loka's wings pulled tighter. "No one stole anything."

"No?" Clarence's smile moved, but his eyes did not. "Your finest note. The room forgot your name." He let the sentence breathe. "They called it worship. I call it overshadowing."

The word lodged in Loka's ribs like a shard. He tried to breathe around it and could not. In his mind, the memory shifted, tilted a degree, until his joy, still bright, also looked smaller, like a jewel set under a larger jewel's light.

Clarence neither pressed nor relented; he simply walked beside the wound and spoke to it as if to an old friend.

"They do this," he whispered. "They take radiance and fold it under radiance, as though light can only be holy when it hides. They tell you it is humility. I tell you it is fear with a hymn book."

Loka closed his eyes and saw Bruce's tears again, and Philo's fists pressed to his face as if he could hold his heart inside by force. He wanted to call their names, to anchor himself with them. But guilt had a gravity. So did flattery. He felt both.

Clarence gestured almost idly at the corridors of space around them. Far off, the stars dimmed as if they did not wish to be part of the conversation.

"You heard them, you know," Clarence continued. "The lilies curling, the vines recoiling, the river holding its breath. Creation recognizes crowns before courts do. When you passed, the world paused. Not with dread." He tilted his head. "With recognition."

Loka's voice came hoarse. "Recognition of what?"

"Of hierarchy," Clarence said simply. "Of rank. Of right. They will call it blasphemy; I call it math. Your brilliance does not bow; it organizes other lights. That is what a star does. It gathers orbits."

He let the thought sit until it cooled into something that felt like reason.

"Then why," Loka asked, almost to himself, "do I feel like a prison just closed around me?"

Clarence did not smile this time. He honored the question. "Because what they call love was never meant to make you small. Because the Son wears His crown as though none else could be worthy of one. Because what you gave was folded under what He is. And you," he said, laying two fingers lightly against Loka's chest, a mockery of a blessing, "you ache beneath it. There is a name for that ache."

Loka did not ask for it, but the word came anyway.

"Buried greatness."

The dark answered with a long, thin echo.

Loka stood very still. He thought of the first day the harp had been placed in his hands by nothing less than a Voice. He thought of singing and feeling like the song was not going up only, but outward, like rivers turning to roads where others could walk. He thought of the moment in the Hall when he whispered to the Giver of Sound, and the world remembered joy.

"It was not my joy," he said. "It was His."

"Why not both?" Clarence asked so gently it almost sounded devout. "Did He make you an instrument or a fountain? Instruments are played. Fountains feed."

A thin crack ran through the argument, but it ran in a direction Loka wanted. He followed it.

Clarence read it in his posture, the way a hunter reads brush. He let silence bloom again—his favorite medium—and then seeded it with a smaller thought, too small to seem dangerous.

"They will tell you this is testing," he said. "That you should endure and be content. But faithfulness is the song of the content. You were not born for contentment. You were born for wonder. For brilliance that organizes other brilliance. Not chorus, choirmaster."

The last word rang in Loka like a bell struck in an empty church. He steadied himself against a seam of night that felt, absurdly, like a column.

"I only ever wanted to be faithful," he said, and hated the way it sounded: thin, like an apology.

Clarence's answer was not a laugh; it was worse. It was a pitying exhale that made faithfulness sound like a childhood he had outgrown.

"Faithful to what?" he asked. "To a ceiling? To a place where your best becomes preface?"

He did not wait for an answer. He changed the sky.

"Consider this instead: faithful to calling. Faithful to the architecture of what was put in you and never recalled. 'For the gifts and calling of God are without repentance.' He does not take them back. If He will not retrieve them, who told you not to use them?"

Loka thought of the harp again. He thought of how, even now, his hands wanted to find strings and make a road out of sound. He thought of the grief in the Garden, and he thought of how grief, with enough heat under it, becomes resolve.

They walked on, deeper into the hush, until the edges of the Garden were not even rumor. The corridors widened. The light went from dim to silver to something like smoke. The map thinned.

A memory lunged at him without warning: the Son at the foot of the stair, the Holy Adviser veiled beside Him, the Voice from beyond time, saying, "This is My Son, in whom I am well pleased." The whole Hall, like a single knee, bent.

"Do you hate Him?" Loka asked suddenly. "The Son."

"I do not waste hate," Clarence replied. "It is a poor currency. I prefer leverage."

"And I," Loka said slowly, surprised to hear the truth arrive with the sentence, "do not know what I feel anymore."

"Then I will tell you," Clarence said, and for the first time a little of his impatience showed, the edge of the teacher who has waited long enough for the student to agree. "You feel small where you should feel crowned. You feel necessary and treated like decoration. You feel used to point at another light when your own was given to point at futures."

The last word landed differently. Futures.

"What futures?" Loka asked.

Clarence lifted a hand, and the far veil thinned until it showed a scatter of living worlds like lanterns in mist.

"Those," he said. "The Third and the Fifth, and the ones beyond the fold you have not yet named. Places where questions are already awake. Places where wonder is not taught as obedience but as breath. If you will not be crowned here, be crowned there. Not with conquest. Not yet. With questions. With permission."

He smiled now, not with triumph but with appetite. "We will not confront the Throne, Loka. We will out-sing it."

They stood for a long while without speaking. Loka's wings loosened a fraction, not in peace but in decision. He lifted his eyes, and in the distance, one world pulsed faintly like a heartbeat. He wondered what their songs sounded like. He wondered what would happen if he told them that glory could be shared like bread and passed hand to hand until no one could tell who had baked it first.

Behind him, the memory of the Hall opened its mouth to warn him, but the dark moved like a curtain and the sound did not carry.

"Before," Clarence said, almost conversational, "you asked about prisons. Shall I name yours?"

Loka did not answer.

"It is not the Hall. Not the Adviser. Not even the Son. Your prison is the word back." Clarence gave it a little bow as if to a failed king. "You keep wanting a seat that is no longer yours. It was never large enough to begin with."

He extended his hand, palm up, the way one does to a skittish animal.

"Forward," he said. "Only forward."

For the first time, Loka looked at Clarence's hand without flinching. He did not take it. But he did not refuse it either. Something in him stepped without feet.

They moved again, a little faster now. The corridors of shadowlight became paths; the paths became lanes; the lanes became something like roads. Clarence spoke of methods, of audiences, of soft entries. He spoke of questions that look like praise and praise that tastes like doubt. He spoke of slogans.

"Fair to One," he tried on his tongue, as if testing a lyric, "Unfair to All."

Loka did not repeat it, but the phrase circled and would not leave.

"Not armies," Clarence said, "stories. Not swords, slogans. A campaign carried on the wind. By the time they hear it at the Hall, they will call it blasphemy, but they will be arguing with echoes."

Loka stopped. "And if I am wrong?"

Clarence's eyes softened with a tenderness that had the exact weight of a net. "Then you will have done what you were made to do: you will have led. Even your error will have magnitude. But you are not wrong."

He stepped closer, lowering his voice until the dark leaned in to listen.

"Listen to me. You cannot go back to the Garden yet. If you do, they will smother you with pity and call it love. Pity is a slow coffin. Forward with me, and your ache becomes architecture."

Loka's face changed at that. There was a piece of him that had always loved building; arranging sound until people could walk on it. Architecture. The word fit too well.

They reached a ridge of crystal, black and gleaming, that overlooked a bloom of distant stars. The Third World pulsed again, closer now, blue-hued and young. Between here and there lay the lanes Clarence had spoken of: lightless highways where words travel faster than wings.

Loka spoke first. "We go softly."

Clarence inclined his head. "Like wind through the garden."

"Word by word," Loka said.

"World by world," Clarence finished, pleased.

A new silence fell, lighter than the one behind them, heavier than the one ahead. The kind of silence two conspirators share without shame.

Loka looked down at his hands. For a moment he expected a

harp to appear as it always had, at a whisper. Nothing came. The strings were not gone; they had moved to his throat. He sang a single note too low to hear, too real to ignore. The pathway to the Third World trembled as if something inside it recognized its maker.

Behind them, far away where light still remembered its manners, the Holy Adviser turned his head without knowing why. In the Hall, Bruce lifted his face and did not like the taste of the air. Philo's hands closed as if to catch something he could not name.

Clarence watched Loka and nodded once, satisfied.

"Forward," he said, a benediction and a dare.

Loka did not answer with words. He stepped.

The corridor before them unrolled like parchment receiving a royal decree. The Third World brightened as if someone had whispered, "Be ready."

They went not as invaders, but as tutors. Not with banners, but with questions. The dark parted like a curtain being trained to applause.

Just before the veil took them, Loka looked back. The memory of the Hall rose again, of the Son, the stair, and the Voice, and for a breath he was certain he would turn. He did not turn. He only blinked.

A star behind them dimmed, as though it could not bear to watch.

They entered the lanes.

And somewhere deep in the architecture of Heaven, a script that had not been read in ages began to glow.

Prepare.

CHAPTER FIFTEEN

The Council of Creatures

The hush of heaven bled into the land. It wasn't silence the way night falls silent when the crickets pause. It was thicker, heavier, like the pause of a held breath. The river ran, but slower, as though weighed down. The leaves of the forest drooped like tired arms. Even the stars above blinked warily, reluctant to shine.

At the edge of the Colossal City, where the river poured bright and steady, the guardians were already at their post. Captain D stood like a polished spear, fins flaring like banners, his scales flashing silver and blue in the moonlight. Behind him stretched the Fish Army: minnows in tight clusters, carp in shining rows, trout gleaming like arrows, and bass holding the line like stubborn sentries.

"Hold formation!" Captain D barked, his deep voice carrying across the water. "No stragglers. No slackers. Tight tails, proud fins! We represent the river. Dignity, even if you're a guppy."

A small guppy in the front row quivered and squeaked, "Yes, sir! Proud fins!" before promptly swimming in the wrong direction. The row behind him broke into bubbles of laughter until Captain D snapped, "Eyes front!" The laughter subsided into muffled giggles.

Even in the heaviness, there was life. That was the way of the river.

THE DRAGON'S WARNING

From the shadows beneath the trees came the low scrape of scales against bark, tail dragging furrows into the earth. The ground trembled as Syracuse, the ancient dragon, emerged into the clearing. His eyes, one half-shut, one gleaming sharp, studied the river, and the army arrayed before it.

"The air tastes wrong," he said at last, voice like shifting stone. "Bitter, like ash before fire. This silence is not peace. It is warning."

A ripple of unease passed through the gathering. Fishtails flicked nervously. The trees seemed to lean closer to listen.

At the four corners of the clearing, shadows moved: the Lions. They padded into position, silent, regal, their wings folded, their eyes glowing like golden embers. They did not speak, but their presence was enough. The weight of guardianship settled over the place.

Overhead, the steady circle of Liberty's wings carved through the sky. She did not land yet, but the wind off her feathers stirred the clearing, rustling leaves, sending ripples across the river. Her watch was unbroken, eyes in every direction.

HELMETS AND HUMOR

And then, as if the hush itself invited interruption, came the sound of tumbling, scrambling, and two unmistakable voices.

"Wait, wait, hold up! My helmet's on backwards again!"

"You're fine. Helmets are helmets. Front, back, sideways, it's still a helmet."

Grace and Mercy stumbled out of the forest and into the clearing, each wearing a helmet far too large for their wombat-like heads. Mercy's (the boy's) sat cockeyed, slipping over one ear, while Grace's (the girl's) was upside down, chin strap dangling uselessly.

Mercy puffed out his chest. "Well, when it goes down, I'm ready. Got my helmet, got my courage, and just enough dinner left in my belly to keep me fierce."

Grace tugged at her upside-down helmet and added solemnly, "Yeah, ready to fight...though I'd feel better if someone told me what we're fighting."

The Fish Army erupted in bubbles of laughter. A guppy in the back squeaked, "Hear, hear!"

Captain D spun around, scandalized. "Silence in the ranks!"

Which, of course, only made more snickers ripple through the water. Even Syracuse's massive jaw curled in the faintest smirk.

A VOICE OF PROPHECY

From the treeline came a soft glow, like moonlight carried on hooves. A unicorn stepped into the clearing, its mane shimmering with faint starlight, horn gleaming like polished silver. Its eyes were deep pools, reflecting sorrow and hope together.

"When the song breaks," the unicorn said, voice as calm as water over stone, "even silence must choose a side."

The words fell like a stone in still water, rippling outward through the creatures. Fish flicked their tails. The Lions' eyes burned brighter. Syracuse lowered his head in respect.

Grace tilted her helmet and whispered, "That sounded serious."

Mercy, nodding too vigorously, added, "Well, we choose the side with snacks and no lies."

Laughter cracked through the heaviness, awkward but real. And somehow, the truth in the wombats' words landed heavier than the jest.

THE MULTITUDES ARRIVE

Then the forest itself began to stir. Leaves rustled. Branches shook. And from every path and thicket, creatures poured into the clearing:

- Stag-horned owls with antlers like branching chandeliers, their eyes luminous.
- Long-eared hares dragging bundles of herbs and roots.
- Tortoises with glowing shells, pulsing faintly like lanterns

in the dark.

- Fox-birds, tiny creatures with wings and tails like flames, flitting from branch to branch.
- Stone-backed badgers, their steps heavy as grinding rock.
- Great elk, heads crowned with moss and ivy.
- Even the tiny beetles came, shimmering in emerald clusters along the ground.

The clearing filled until it hummed with breath and movement. A multitude of the land, river, and sky, gathered at the river's edge. And then, softly at first, then louder, they began to chant. Not in solemn liturgy, but in a playful, defiant rhythm, like a child's rhyme:

Truth will stand, lies will fall,

We'll cheer the King who rules them all!

The chant spread. Owls hooted, hares thumped, fox-birds whistled. The Fish Army thrummed their tails in rhythm, a watery drumline to the song. Grace and Mercy joined in at once, Mercy way off beat, Grace shouting far too loud.

The air shifted. The hush was still there, but it wasn't suffocating. It was alive, filled with defiance and laughter. Syracuse rumbled, a deep chuckle that shook the ground. "Well, if war comes, at least it won't be quiet."

THE WEIGHT RETURNS

The chant faded as Liberty descended at last. She landed with wings spread wide, feathers catching the dim light, eyes all around her head gleaming like stars. She surveyed the gathering: river, forest, field, sky.

Her voice carried like thunder restrained: "The heavens stir. The earth quakes. The choice is near."

The Lions did not move, but their eyes flared, casting light like torches.

Captain D raised his chin, chest swelling with pride. "Then the river will hold," he declared. "No shadow crosses without account!" His army flicked tails in unison, the sound like a hundred drums.

The unicorn lowered its head, horn glimmering faintly. "So it begins," it whispered.

Syracuse lifted his massive head, his one open eye blazing. "Then let the creatures remember their places, to witness, to wait, to stand."

The hush returned, heavy but holy. Helmets no longer looked so funny. The chant still echoed faintly in the trees, like a promise carried on the wind. And the clearing, full of fish and fox-birds, lions and wombats, dragons and unicorns, stood together, a council of creatures, waiting on the edge of history.

CHAPTER SIXTEEN

The Silence in Heaven

And all of heaven stood at half-mast, not by command, nor ceremony, but by something deeper: an instinct in the very stones of the courts and the wings of the host. Light dimmed, not out of fear, but out of grief. The banners that had once rippled in the breath of joy now hung heavy, as though the sky itself refused to dance.

The Place Called Beautiful, which had known endless music, was suddenly still. Angels paused mid-flight, their wings folding as if even the air had grown heavy. Songs caught in throats, instruments hung quiet in hands. The golden halls that once rang with worship now echoed with a kind of sacred hush; a silence not empty, but brimming with mourning.

The hush pressed down upon the glass rivers, slowing their current. The jeweled gardens wilted as though bowing. Even the stars above blinked cautiously, their light paling, as though reluctant to shine.

At the edge of the Hall of Lights, the Holy Advisor stood, his robe still bright but his eyes darkened. He felt it first, before word had traveled, before Bruce and Philo returned, before the stars themselves quivered. Something had been torn. Not slain, but lost. Not forgotten, but fallen.

And in the garden below, two angels knelt with their faces to the ground, their tears seeping into the soil that once knew only laughter. Bruce, usually steady, was silent and still. Philo trembled with a sorrow that had no words left to speak.

Somewhere above, even the Seraphim folded their wings.

And God said nothing. Not out of absence, but because some moments are so holy, so heartbreaking, that even Heaven must wait.

THE RETURN

The sound of footsteps broke the hush in the Hall of Lights. Bruce and Philo entered like men returning from war, not with victory, but with smoke on their wings and grief in their bones. Their stride was heavy, their shoulders bowed. They carried neither banners nor trophies. Only loss.

Christian stood beside the Holy Advisor, who had not moved since the first silence fell. The young warrior's jaw tightened, his eyes already knowing the truth, though he longed to deny it.

Bruce spoke first, his voice low and raw. "He's gone."

Christian's brow furrowed. "Gone? Where?"

"Not gone, gone," Philo said, stepping forward, his accent thick with grief. His eyes were red and raw, his breath uneven, "but lost all the same. We saw it in his eyes. He's not Loka anymore. Not the Loka we knew."

Bruce added quietly, his voice breaking, "Clarence was with him. Walked in beside him like it was nothing. Smooth. Polished. Like he hadn't just helped tear the soul out of Heaven."

Philo's hands shook as he balled them into fists. "That slick tongue of his, all syrup and smile. Like he's just here for a stroll. But we know. We know now."

The Holy Advisor's face was grave, unmoving, his ancient eyes searching echoes beyond the room. Christian turned toward him, desperate.

"Advisor...what do you see?"

The old one spoke slowly, each word weighted like stone. "I see an ancient thread woven into new cloth. A trickery older than this realm. A masterstroke of pride, disguised as destiny, wrapped in flatteries and false wisdom." His gaze shifted toward the distant garden, now silent. "This is the work of Sin Say."

Bruce's eyes widened. "The Deceiver?"

Philo nearly spat the name. "The same who stirs rebellion with honey and dresses poison like prophecy."

Christian's shoulders squared, resolve hardening. "And now he has Loka."

The Advisor nodded, voice like thunder muffled by sorrow. "Yes. He has a foothold, and from it, he will rise. Not with war drums, but with whispers. With promises. With half-truths."

Bruce lowered his head, fists clenching tighter. "We tried. We begged him."

Philo shook his head, voice cracking. "Didn't matter. He'd already decided. We were talkin' to his face, but his heart was already walkin' away."

The Hall of Lights itself seemed to darken, as if its very beams grieved with them.

Christian broke the silence, his voice steady but heavy. "Then the war has begun. Not the one with swords. The war of hearts. Of choice. And we will not lose another."

The Advisor's robe whispered across the marble as he turned. "Then let us prepare. The days of division have come. And every light must now choose what it will burn for."

THE REVELATION

Far beyond the garden, beyond the Place Called Beautiful, the dark corridors of space rippled. Clarence and Loka stepped through the final portal, into a realm far from the sacred heart of Heaven. What once felt like exile now felt like stage lights.

Clarence walked a half-step ahead, his grin sharp, his voice like velvet soaked in poison. "Atta-boy, Loka," he purred darkly. "You sure showed 'em. The holy ones, the meek-minded masses. You declared yourself tonight. Finally."

Loka said nothing. His eyes still glowed faintly, not with holy light, but with residue, like an ember twisted.

Clarence twirled, walking backward to face him. "You're the boss now, my young Prince of the Air. No more whispers. No more shadows. We're done hiding. But we can't stay here."

He stopped at the edge of a black ridge overlooking a galaxy in motion, stars burning, worlds spinning, systems aligning.

"Oh, we'll come back," Clarence promised, arms spreading wide. "And when we do...it'll all be yours. Every gate, every garden, every glory." His grin widened like a mask cracking open. "But first...we have to campaign."

Loka raised an eyebrow, curiosity flickering faintly behind the fog.

"The largest one the Federation's ever seen," Clarence said. "Every world, every creature, every corner of creation is ours for the taking. Not by force, not at first. No, no. We sow doubt. We plant ambition. We feed that sacred little question: Did God really say...?" He leaned close, eyes sharp as obsidian. "You want a slogan? I've got a beauty: Fair to One, Unfair to All."

Loka blinked. "What?"

Clarence's voice dropped lower, venom rich. "Think about it. He gave one Son everything. All the glory. All the power. All the worship. And what did the rest of us get? Orders. Obedience. Chains dressed as loyalty. It's not divine justice. It's divine favoritism."

He began pacing, his words swelling like a storm.

"But no more. We turn the Federation's allegiance. We pull back the veil. We show them the truth. And from every star and every system, we will gather them. Until we've built not just a rebellion," he stopped and faced Loka fully, eyes blazing like fallen stars. "but a kingdom."

The silence that followed was not peace. It was the pause before thunder.

Clarence spoke again, softly now, like a serpent coiling. "There must be war in the heavens." Then, louder, arms raised in triumph: "And we will win."

He turned to Loka, smiling like a false god. "We. Will. Win."

The stars seemed to hold their breath.

Loka stood silent, staring at the one he had once called Clarence. The grin sharpened. The eyes gleamed with something eternal and wrong.

"Oh, by the way," Clarence said, his voice smooth as silk over glass, "you can call me Sin Say."

Loka flinched. "You mean the ancient deceiver...of old?"

Sin Say's smile stretched wider, darker. "The one and only." He spun slowly, arms outstretched like a maestro orchestrating chaos. "But names are nothing. Titles rise and fall. Power remains."

His hand pressed against Loka's chest, over the ember of his calling.

"You still carry it, you know. What He gave you. The music. The fire. The light that once led worship in Heaven's courts. He gave it without recall. No refunds. No strings."

He leaned closer, whispering like a curse: "For the gifts and calling of God are without repentance."

Something in Loka shuddered. It was true. Even in his fall, even in his bitterness, the gifts remained. Untouched. Unreturned. Holy tools now wielded for unholy ends.

So the two vanished into the shadow lanes and lightless highways of the galaxies. Not with armies, not with weapons, but with words and wonders. Sin Say, deceiver of old ,and Loka, once the voice of worship, now a siren of sedition.

And the heavens trembled.

THE TRUMPET

Back in the Hall of Lights, the silence broke. A trumpet rang out, clear, golden, terrible. Its sound cut through the marble, through the heavens, through the very bones of creation.

All of Heaven assembled. Millions upon millions of angels stood in rank and file. Creatures of every kind filled the chamber:

Syracuse the dragon, wings folded in solemnity; Captain D with his fish army arrayed like silver phalanxes; Grace and Mercy, helmets now tucked under their arms, unusually quiet; and Liberty, eagle of justice, her wings stretching from horizon to horizon.

At the head stood the Holy Advisor, aged as eternity, robed in light. He looked not at the multitude, but at the Throne.

At the silent nod of the Creator and the Son, he turned and spoke. His voice thundered with restrained fire: "War is coming."

A gasp, not of fear, but of realization, rippled through the host.

"Not for territory. Not for thrones. But for the hearts of all creation." His eyes swept the vast assembly, his voice deepening. "Ready yourselves. The silence is ending. The days of choice are upon us. Every wing, every flame, every star must decide."

The word thundered through the cosmos.

Prepare.

Stars flared.

Swords shimmered.

Wings unfolded.

And somewhere in the dark between galaxies, Sin Say smiled, not at the word, but at the

war it promised.

The word itself rippled outward through roots and rivers, through forests and peaks, through sea armies and star fields. It whispered on wings and burned in breath. It became not just a command, but a current.

For the song had changed, and soon, the silence between notes would be broken...by war.

CHAPTER SEVENTEEN

The Quiet Campaign

There were no gates at the Edge of Darkness, only a hush, and the slow sigh of stars that no longer sang. The place was neither night nor day, but something in between: twilight stretched too far, shadowlight lingering too long. Here, where Heaven's warmth faded to silver-grey, two figures stood beneath the veil, their voices soft enough not to echo. Sin Say leaned against a jagged outcrop of crystal, its surface dark as obsidian yet flecked with imprisoned starlight. His one-time grin had settled into something quieter, a smile that never reached the eyes. He scanned the endless expanse before them as if searching for weak points in the canvas of creation.

"There," he said at last, pointing toward a soft constellation that pulsed faintly like a heartbeat. "The Third World. Quiet. Eager. Full of thinkers."

Loka stood beside him, arms folded, wings folded tighter still. His silhouette glowed faintly, but it was not the light of worship anymore; it was residue, the last shimmer of a star already falling.

"And do they still sing the old songs?" His voice was measured, neither warm nor cold.

"They do," Sin Say replied, voice smooth as silk drawn across glass. "But their hearts are open. Not rebellious, just curious like yours once was."

Loka's eyes narrowed. "Curiosity isn't rebellion. It's how truth finds breath."

He stepped forward, and the faint light of the realm behind

them rimmed his form like a false halo. "We won't confront the Throne. Not yet. We go softly. Like wind through the garden. Word by word. World by world."

Sin Say tilted his head. "And when do we return here? To finish what was begun?"

"When the song has changed," Loka answered, "and the echo answers us."

A soft chuckle rolled from Sin Say's throat. He unrolled a slender scroll of shimmering starlight, and words appeared upon it like living fire. Etched in elegant script were the words he had rehearsed:

Fair to One, Unfair to All.

The slogan pulsed faintly, as though the universe itself recoiled at its logic. They stood in silence, two silhouettes at the edge of forever, plotting not a campaign of swords but of syllables.

THE THIRD WORLD

The Third World was young: blue-hued, radiant, shimmering under twin suns that arced across its skies like golden guardians. Its valleys curled like parchment being read for the first time, lush with thought-vines that glowed faintly when touched. Rivers of silverwater bent through plains like living script.

The people of this world were seekers, shaped tall and luminous, eyes wide with wonder. They were philosophers by nature, builders of song and form. Their speech was threaded with music, their questions like offerings placed on altars.

When the two strangers appeared, there were no walls to bar them. The citizens welcomed them with songs woven from their own thought-vines, garlands spun not from flowers but from ideas strung together like pearls.

No fear.

No suspicion.

Only eagerness.

Loka stood tall among them. His wings remained half-furled,

not threatening but impossible to ignore. His presence was as radiant as an echo of Heaven's choir still clinging to him. Even fallen embers give off heat.

He raised a hand, and the crowd hushed. "Brothers," he began, his voice like honey poured slowly, "and thinkers of this good world, you are not bound by silence, are you?"

The people shifted, curious. One voice from the multitude called out, "We seek understanding."

Loka nodded, pausing with the cadence of a teacher who knows the class leans forward to catch every word. "Then I bring you something precious. A thought. A question. Not a command."

He stepped down from the polished rise where he stood, walking among them like rain easing through a grove. His tone lowered, intimate.

"If there is one above all," he said softly, "and we are made in his glory, should not the glory flow freely? Should wisdom not be shared equally, not reserved for one throne alone?"

The people glanced skyward; others at each other. Seeds had been dropped. Behind him, Sin Say remained silent. His role was not to speak, but to study the ripples like a stone dropped in water. Every hesitation, every tilt of the head, he drank it in like a predator memorizing prey.

Loka's voice sank lower, heavy as velvet. "The Son is radiant. Yes. Worthy. Yes. But fair to one...unfair to all." The phrase slipped from his tongue like a pearl, gleaming and poisonous.

A murmur passed through the crowd. Soft. Uneasy. But present.

AMONG THE LISTENERS

Two lingered after the gathering, unwilling to let the words die with the day. They stood beneath glass-barked trees whose leaves caught the twin-sunlight and fractured it into kaleidoscopes of blue and gold. One was named Aiven, a philosopher. His eyes were wide, still shimmering with the reflection of Loka's presence.

The other, Calith, was a singer and scribe, her voice known among her people as one that could steady storms.

Aiven exhaled, trembling with excitement. "Did you feel it, Calith? The weight of his words? It wasn't speech; it was revelation."

Calith plucked thoughtfully at a vine curling near her wrist, its glow fading and brightening like breath. "It was eloquent," she admitted, "but eloquence can be a veil. He spoke of freedom, but did not name the chains."

Aiven turned to her, surprised. "But don't you see? He offers us dignity. Shared radiance. No more lesser lights orbiting one sun."

Calith's gaze lifted toward the heavens. "And yet, it was the one sun that called us into being. Do you trust a fire that has left the hearth?"

Her words hung in the air like a chord unresolved. Silence stretched between them.

Aiven whispered softer now. "He spoke as if he cared for all, but I could not tell if he loved any."

Calith's voice grew gentler, but firmer. "Then we must think, not just feel."

The wind through the glass-barked trees seemed to agree, whispering back her words like an echo: *think, not just feel.*

THE WHISPER AND THE WATCHER

High above, unseen to the citizens, Sin Say watched the dialogue from the shadows of the ridge. He smiled faintly. Division always began in whispers, not wars. Aiven had swallowed the pearl. Calith resisted, but resistance itself would keep the question alive.

He turned to Loka. "You see? With a single phrase, already it grows legs. That's the beauty of it. Words walk farther than armies."

Loka's eyes stayed on the crowd dispersing. "Words endure when they are true."

Sin Say's grin tightened. "And when they are almost true."

SEEDS OF SEDITION

The campaign spread quietly. Not with horns or banners, but with questions. One listener carried it to his home, another to her circle, another to a gathering at the silverwater's edge. Each retelling polished the phrase until it gleamed.

Fair to One, Unfair to All.

It became a riddle, a puzzle, a chant hummed under breath. Not shouted, but whispered in corners where curiosity met doubt.

The Third World did not fall in a day. Worlds never do. But it bent. Slightly. Enough to show the strain.

And in the Edge of Darkness, Sin Say folded the starlight scroll and smiled. "The campaign has begun."

CHAPTER EIGHTEEN

The Final Campaign

They traveled far beyond the known stars, past familiar constellations that had guided pilgrim worlds for ages, past the old songs sung beneath auroras, past even the hush where light itself seemed to listen. Loka moved like a dark comet through these reaches: bright to those who admired his former radiance, shadow to those who felt a change they could not name. He murmured, almost reverently, to the hosts of many spheres, and they, surprised by his courtesy and the gravity in his voice, leaned in.

He never called it rebellion. Not yet. He asked for readiness. For vigilance. For a steadying of ranks in case the cosmos shifted. He asked if they had ever wondered why one decree stood above the rest, why one throne could not be questioned, why one name, though lovely, must never be weighed or tested by noble minds. He asked if love did not sometimes require brave counsel.

And Sin Say, close as breath but still apart, smiled.

"Soft tread now. Give them a gallant reason. They love gallantry almost as much as truth."

THE WORLDS HE VISITED

They arrived first at a world with silver oceans and moon-flowers that opened only to hymns. The angels there bore filaments of light woven into their garments like living embroidery. They had studied mercy so long that even their rebukes felt like a warm blanket. Loka spoke on a terrace that faced two suns. He praised their devotion, named their virtues, and asked a single question that sounded like a blessing.

"Is there not, in all benevolence, room for counsel with the Highest? For a convening of the wise before decrees are sealed?"

The terrace murmured. One captain lifted a hand, more curious than offended. "To question is the beginning of worship here, Light-bearer. But to overthrow..."

"To overthrow?" Loka laughed softly. "I spoke only of readiness! In case the heavens sway."

"Good," Sin Say breathed, close as breath but still apart. "Give them a shadow and let them supply the fear."

From there they crossed to an old and settled sphere where the night-forests sang with memory. The angels there wore bark-brown coats and braided the names of the humble into their belts. They guarded stories like jewels. On a ridge above their city, Loka sat by their fire and told a parable about a vineyard whose branches grew so thick with fruit that the trellis creaked.

"Would you shore the beams if they groaned?" he asked.

Heads nodded.

"And if the Owner said, 'Leave it be,' though the crack widened?"

The firelight found complicated faces. Someone whispered, "The Owner knows."

"Indeed," Loka said kindly. "And yet...love sometimes sends carpenters with hammers."

The third passage took them near a young world still warm with a first dawn. The angels, newly minted and bright as struck flint, were eager to serve and eager to think. Loka did not press them. He simply admired their order, remarked on how they listened to each other, and asked if they practiced listening up with the same deliberation.

When they said yes, he commended them. And when they asked what he meant by listening up, he only smiled and said, "Sometimes a throne speaks easiest to those who can frame good questions."

"Questions loosen joints," Sin Say murmured, close as breath but still apart. "Soon they will pivot for you without feeling the turn."

THE HUNGER GROWS

It was not enough.

Loka gathered attentive minds and brave hearts from the edges of many skies, but he was restless still. The ache was not sated by numbers. It burned hotter with each pledge, like a fire fed by offerings that strangely made the blaze hungrier. He wanted voices from the Kingdom Realm, from the Place Called Beautiful, from the Garden itself where the River of Life curled like a smile. He wanted the throne not merely to tremble, but to be emptied.

Sin Say's chuckle was a purr of coals, close as breath but still apart.

"There it is: the true hunger. Say it plainly to yourself, if not to them. You do not want applause; you want station."

On a crystal waystation between spheres, he met a veteran angel patrol returning from shepherding comets. Their leader, hair like frost, eyes like the deep portion of a well, studied Loka's face with the kind of politeness that comes from old discipline.

"You smell like missing light," she said, not unkindly.

The patrol shifted, startled by her candor.

"I have been far," Loka replied. "Starlight clings and leaves by turns."

"Hmm." She touched the edge of her spear, a ceremonial motion more than a threat.

"You were the one who taught us to sing the First Joy. I wondered, why are you so quiet about joy now?"

"Joy matures," he said. "Some songs require a lower key."

Her gaze did not waver.

"And some songs require truth even when the harmony is tempting."

They parted courteously. Loka did not look back, but the old ache bit like frost inside his ribs.

"She scented you," Sin Say warned, close as breath but still apart. "Even the polite will resist if they smell the real ambition. Garnish your appeal with sorrow; sorrow persuades where power alarms."

So Loka spoke of burdens. He spoke of how the cosmos was vast and how mandates, however perfect, could feel heavy upon worlds still learning tenderness. He spoke of bearing load with the Highest, of standing faithful and sturdy at His right as wise counselors, the sort who listen and, when needed, speak. He never named the throne he wanted. He drew only an outline for others to color as their hopes suggested.

And the recruits came first in twos and tens, then in careful dozens. Not the reckless, mostly; rather the prudent who could be convinced that caution was bravery in a different coat. Ready, they called it. Balanced. Measured. Only a few used a shorter word in their private thoughts: doubt.

BRUCE AND PHILO BEGIN TO WATCH

Word filtered back, as words always do, to the Place Called Beautiful. Some heard and smiled sadly, trusting the Creator to answer winds with whisper and thunder at His time. Others pricked up their ears and wondered how counsel could be wrong if offered in love. And still others, Bruce and Philo among them, went very quiet and began to look for Loka's wake among the stars.

"Do we go to him?" Philo asked, scratching his jaw as if he could rub a simple answer out of it. He smelled of river spray and iron, like a forge that also knew how to fish.

"In time," Bruce said, pushing his spectacles higher though they never fell. He carried the weight of libraries in his sentences. "Let him speak first the word he dares not say. The Creator is patient with us; we must be patient with our brother."

"Brother's ridin' two horses," Philo muttered. "Won't end well."

"Soon," Sin Say humored Loka, close as breath but still apart. "We go home. Take what you want most from the place that made you."

COUNTERFEIT STARS

They returned beneath a sky so clear that the stars looked like bells you could ring with the edge of your nail. The Place Called Beautiful stretched below, its gardens glistening, towers catching the first silver of night, rivers saying soft things to their banks. Loka stood upon a ledge in a region near to the Great Garden but far enough to be alone.

Above him was a spray of stars so perfect that his breath caught not with piety, but with the memory of what he had once loved without envy.

He lifted his palm and made a gesture. At first, the stars did not answer. Then, by subtler means, counterfeit lights patterned the sky. Pale mimics braided through the real constellations, as if a second hand had laid a thin tracing paper over the firmament and drawn ambition where humility had once been. They did not shine so much as suggest. They arranged themselves in a crown too angular for love.

"Practice," Sin Say whispered, close as breath but still apart. "Make the night say what your mouth will."

Loka let the false crown hang there, unsolid, nearly nothing, but enough for his eyes to acclimate to a different map. He closed his eyes and felt the ache, no longer a bite but a throb, not cold but hot. He thought of the pledge of the newly brave, of the courteous soldier's question, of the veteran's spear. He thought of the mount of assembly, and a name came to him like iron warmed in a forge: Zaphon.

He spoke then, not only to the whisper and not only to the stars, but into the great listening that lives behind all ceilings:

I will ascend to the heavens;
I will raise my throne above the stars of God;
I will sit enthroned on the mount of assembly,
on the utmost heights of Mount Zaphon.
I will ascend above the tops of the clouds;
I will make myself like the Most High.
(Isaiah 14:13–14)

The words were older than his mouth and heavier than his lungs. They did not clang; they landed. The air seemed to harden around them. Somewhere very far away, a gate remembered how to close. Somewhere very near, a lily folded up for the night sooner than it had planned.

Sin Say laughed with a low, triumphant sound, close as breath but still apart.

"There. Put a crown on it, son. At last you've said what you want. Now make the world dress to your measure."

THE CONFRONTATION

The sky did not answer with thunder. That would come later. Instead, something subtler happened: the real stars dimmed their chatter, as if courtesy demanded that lesser lights be quiet while a small pride made a large speech. Silence moved out from Loka in slow circles, the kind that make creatures look up without knowing why.

He breathed once, like a swimmer who has decided he can grow gills if he must, and turned from the counterfeits to face the Garden. He saw the Great River glint through trees. He saw the path where Grace and Mercy sometimes walked, nudging hearts with their soft, comical wisdom. He saw the high towers gilded faintly by night. He imagined them empty.

"Beautiful," he said, and the word was not praise but appetite.

"Ugly," said a voice behind him, wry, blunt, country as ever. "Ugly as a stump full o' wasps."

Loka did not startle. He knew that voice better than the shape of his own shadow. He turned, and there they were, framed by honest night: Philo, broad-shouldered as a barn door, and Bruce, luminous with that quiet strength that makes libraries feel like sanctuaries. They had not come roaring. They had come like friends do: late, because love is patient; early, because love is urgent.

Bruce spoke first, as was right.

"Brother," he said, and the word was a mercy. "You have been far. You have gathered counsel from many worlds and returned with a proposal."

"Readiness," Loka replied, spreading his hands as if to bless them. The counterfeit lights behind him tilted, almost proud. "Wisdom. A shared yoke."

Philo spat into the shadows, not disrespectfully, but clearing room for honesty.

"Shared yoke means two oxen pullin' same way. You ain't pullin' His way."

A thin smile touched Loka's mouth. "Have I contradicted a single law? Have I urged the tender to cruelty, the faithful to betrayal? I have asked the brave to stand nearer the throne for counsel fitting princes."

Bruce's eyes softened with grief.

"You have asked for the throne, by another name."

The ache flared. Loka felt the whisper stir, close as breath but still apart. "Let him quote a rule; you quote a vision."

He lifted his chin and gestured to the false crown painted into the sky. "Tell me this is not fitting for one who has borne more light than most. Tell me it is sin to ask whether love might widen its council to include those who have watched its work intimately and long."

Bruce did not look at the counterfeit at all. He looked at Loka. "You are not asking to widen counsel. You are asking to replace trust with influence. They are not the same animal."

Philo stepped up beside Bruce, boots sure on the ledge. "You got the words of a shepherd and the eyes of a wolf right now, friend. That's the kind o' mix that gets lambs goin' the wrong way, 'cause the voice sounds right while the teeth glint."

The laugh came again, close as breath but still apart. "They insult, you inspire. Make your appeal to the noble in them; noble folk are easiest to turn if they think they're guarding something higher."

"Look," Loka said, gentling his tone to near-prayer, "the worlds tremble. You've seen it. Fear in tender places, zeal without knowledge in strong ones. Must we not prepare for the day when the Highest asks us to stand in council for His sake? To hold the beams while the vineyard groans?"

Bruce's answer came as a chord: humble, steady, ancient. "He did not ask for beams when He spun the worlds from nothing. He did not ask for counsel when He hung the laws by which kindness breathes or rivers know their way. And if He had asked, brother, you would not have been there, nor I. We came after the first music. Our first duty is to remember the tune."

Philo nodded. "Also, lemme say it plain so I can hear myself: you're pitchin' a tent on a mountain that ain't yours. That Zaphon name you said? Folks go climbin' there, they come down with frostbite o' the soul."

Loka's mouth tightened. "You heard me."

"We did," Bruce said. "The heavens did, too."

For a moment, no one moved. The counterfeit lights throbbed faintly, as if proud of being noticed. Somewhere beyond the ledge, the River gave a small, contented sigh, as rivers do when they are not worried. Loka found the sound offensive and did not know why.

"Go back," Bruce said softly. "Not to disgrace. There is none while breath remains. Not to shame. Love does not ration itself that way. Go back to the place where your first joy lived. Find the hymn that does not need a throne to make it sing."

Philo leaned forward, hands on his belt. "And if you can't

remember the hymn, borrow mine. It ain't pretty, but it's true. 'He's the Maker; I ain't.' That little tune'll save your life when the big songs get complicated."

The whisper pressed, close as breath but still apart. "They are small men, even if they're tall. They speak of hymns while you speak of governance. They speak of remembering while you speak of destiny. Give them your back; give the worlds your face."

"Brothers," Loka said, and the word was as smooth as polished stone, "I thank you. Truly. But the hour is later than you know, and the cosmos larger. A single voice, no matter how lovely, should not carry every verdict."

Bruce's eyes shone. "That single voice spoke stars into speech and taught oceans their grammar. He is not merely lovely; He is Lord."

"Then," Loka replied, and the angle of his head made the counterfeit crown align exactly with his brow, "let Him prove it against counsel."

Philo's jaw bunched. "I don't like where you're standin', son."

"Nor I," Bruce said, pain in the words like a violin string pulled hard. "But I love you where you are. And because I do, hear this: the path from readiness to rebellion is shorter than a sigh. You have already taken most of it by calling distrust wisdom and appetite calling itself justice."

The sky stirred, almost shyly, like a curtain catching a draft. Loka felt the world tip under his feet; not physically, but in the way a heart tilts when it has made a choice and all the corridors of consequence begin to align. He breathed in the clean scent of Garden night and found it thin.

"Then let the corridors open," he said, not loudly. "Let counsel gather. Those who would stand near the throne for the sake of the worlds, come. Those who believe love can bear another voice, come. Those who have grown beyond songs meant for infants, come."

Sin Say purred, close as breath but still apart. "Call them

adults. The proud love that word."

Bruce took one step forward, and his voice, though quiet, filled the ledge. "Hear also this call: all who remember the First Music, return to it. All who have mistaken ambition for guardianship, wake. All who have heard our brother and felt something bright and bitter rise within, ask the Highest to name it before you kiss it."

Philo's hand fell to the hilt at his side, not because he meant to strike, but because honest men touch old tools when they're sad.

"I ain't gonna wrestle you tonight," he said to Loka. "I reckon we will all soon enough. But I am gonna say a thing my grandpappy angel told me: 'If you gotta talk yourself into peace, it ain't peace.' Been a lotta talkin' round you lately."

Silence again, thicker now, heavy with prelude.

Loka lifted his gaze to the counterfeit stars. They aligned to his will because he had drawn them so. For a heartbeat he almost laughed at the simplicity of how easy it is to be crowned by your own chalk marks. Then the ache became certainty. He felt the recruits arrayed across the worlds, felt their careful hearts tipping, felt the sweet pull of leadership that does not ask permission.

He lowered his hand and the false crown steadied.

"Go," Bruce said to Philo without taking his eyes from Loka. "Gather those who waver and remind them of the old kindnesses. I will remain."

"No," Loka answered calmly. "You will carry a message."

Philo's eyebrows shot up.

"Oh, we takin' orders now?"

"Tell them," Loka said, voice steady as a plumb line, "that I will ascend. That I will raise my throne above the stars of God."

CHAPTER NINETEEN

The Battle Before Time

THE STILLNESS BEFORE

There are silences that hush the heart, and there are silences that hush the stars. In the Kingdom Realm, the second kind had fallen. The Singing Hills did not sing. Their grasses, once rippling like choirs, lay flat in a wind that refused to rise. The River of Life still moved, but its voice was no longer laughter. It whispered now, as though it carried a secret too heavy to spill. Even the light slowed its journey, sliding across domes and leaves with the careful steps of a priest bearing oil. From the towers of the city to the furthest edges of the Garden, a stillness rested on every leaf, every wing, every ear that could listen.

It was the moment before the first stone tumbles into a canyon, when even echoes lean forward, waiting to be born.

It was the hush before war.

Children of the Colossal City, the bright-eyed tender ones who traced constellations with their fingertips, had been gathered inside. No locks barred the doors (locks had never been needed here), but the thresholds felt tighter, as if even stone braced itself for what was coming. In meadows near the southern walls, lilies fixed their gaze eastward and refused to turn, unwilling to miss the first shadow of the King.

All of creation leaned toward a center.

Heaven held its breath.

SIGNS OF READINESS

Yet even in the hush, movement stirred, not hurried, not noisy, but deliberate, as if the Realm itself knew that haste is a stranger to wisdom.

In the Hall of Shields, golden-armored angels polished helms and strapped on greaves. The sound of metal was not clatter; it was rhythm, like the sound of vows being remembered. Braziers glowed, warming oil that sent out the sober scent of frankincense. This was no festival incense; it was the kind burned in hours of reckoning.

A young sentinel, cheeks still bright with new light, raised his visor and whispered to the captain beside him.

"Will it hurt?"

The captain's eyes softened, though his jaw was firm. "Only pride."

Across the folds of the Singing Hills, where laughter once leapt like deer, long tables held rows of scrolls. Swift scribes sealed them with wax and pressed them into ribbons of light. They were not writing new decrees, but finishing words that had waited since before the first dawn. Each seal gave a faint sigh, as if the parchment itself knew it was going to war. Couriers, slim, bright, and silent, received them, bowed, and vanished into paths of wind no eye could follow.

Beneath the Dome of Light, Michael stood rooted like a spear planted in granite. His eyes were closed, his breath measured, hands steady at his sides. He was not waiting for a sound. He was waiting for a signal; that invisible cue when time itself must step aside and let Eternity pass through.

A young warrior drew near, hesitated, then bowed his head.

"Speak," Michael said without opening his eyes.

"The legions are mustering," the warrior answered. "Some ask if the Song can be torn."

Michael opened his eyes. If galaxies had needed kindling, his gaze alone could have lit them. "Nothing tears the Song," he said. "But it can be refused."

"And if it is refused?"

"Then the Song sings around what will not sing. And what will not sing," Michael said, his voice like granite sliding into place, "learns the weight of silence."

The warrior nodded, throat tight. Even the Dome itself seemed to lean closer, as if it, too, wanted to remember those words.

On the far edge of the Garden, where olive branches bent low to cradle pools of shadow, Philo sat cross-legged on a stone. A whetstone lay in his hand, a long blade across his lap. He pulled steel against stone with slow, unhurried strokes, as though sharpening patience itself. The blade was not made to spill blood. Nothing in the Garden had been shaped for that. It was made to cut lies from truth, shadow from light, noise from voice. Philo tested the edge with his thumb and grunted.

"Not for flesh," he muttered in his country drawl, "but for binding pride to its own chain." He spat in the dust, rubbed it with his palm until the spit made a circle, then kept working.

A small angel crept closer, his feathers still soft as down.

"Sir Philo?" he asked. "Why sharpen a blade that never cuts?"

"Because, little oak," Philo said without looking up, "some chains don't break, they just get revealed." He lifted the blade, caught the morning light along its edge, and nodded. "And when pride sees itself plain, it calls that pain."

The little angel puzzled over this, then sat nearby and began polishing a buckler that had never once been dented.

A SCHOLAR'S GRIEF

Bruce walked alone in the Hall of Records. It was not a hall of shelves, yet shelves were everywhere. Not a hall of books, yet every wall breathed memory. Moments hovered like lanterns in the air, each one trembling with its own soft light. Brush one, and it opened. Whisper to another, and it answered with a picture, a voice, or even a scent. The whole hall hummed like a beehive, alive with the low thrum of history waiting to be noticed.

Bruce's robe whispered across the floor as he reached toward a faint glimmer. His hand passed through it, and a memory flared into being.

He stood again beneath the Starfall Tree.

Loka was there, younger, if such a thing could be said of beings untouched by decay. His laughter rang out, rich and unforced, echoing like bells across silver branches. They had been arguing over a line in an ancient song. Bruce insisted it pointed toward mercy. Loka swore it spoke of honor. Neither won. The argument dissolved into such laughter that the birds overhead scattered, offended by the noise. Loka leaned too far back, mimicking the startled bird, and nearly toppled over. Bruce caught him by the arm, both of them laughing so hard that tears of light streaked their faces.

Bruce reached out, touching that memory as if it were alive. He could almost smell the bark, feel the leaf brushing his shoulder as it fell.

But then the vision dimmed. The laughter grew faint. And he was alone again in the Hall.

He pressed his lips together until they whitened. His voice cracked when he spoke. "You could have had joy forever, brother. Why trade eternity for a shadow? Why chase the outline of a crown when the King's face was your sun?"

The memory lantern flickered, as if to answer, then sank back into its silent orbit.

Somewhere in the distance, a trumpet was being polished. The sound did not reach the hall, yet Bruce felt the shine of it in his bones. He pulled his robe tight, fastening it with firm hands. His back straightened. The time for remembering was over. The Hall was faithful, but it did not beg.

At the threshold, a scribe in moon-colored robes stood waiting. She bowed low and hesitated before speaking.

"Master Bruce, one memory will not sit still. It flutters."

Bruce paused. "Which?"

"The night the lions took their places at the four corners."

"Does it change?"

"It sharpens," she whispered, eyes wide. "As though someone is looking at it closely...from

the other side."

Bruce breathed deep. His answer came steady. "Let it sharpen. Clarity is a kindness, even when it hurts."

He raised two fingers, a blessing she had once taught him, then turned and stepped into the waiting silence of the day.

THE WISE ONE WAKES

Deep in the forest, older than counting, where roots tangled like secrets and the canopy held starlight as if it had been poured into bowls of leaves, a single plume of smoke curled from a cave.

Not the smoke of fire. The smoke of breath. Ancient breath.

Syracuse stirred.

The dragon uncoiled slowly, like a mountain that had decided to remember it could stand. His scales shifted against one another with the sound of porcelain cups clinking in some forgotten banquet hall. Moss fell away in curtains. Pebbles tumbled from ridges of his back as his great body shook the slumber off.

One eye opened, molten, alive, the color of iron in a furnace. The other remained closed, as it ever did, peering into that place between what is and what will be, a place only wisdom can live.

"It has begun," he said. His voice rolled like continents grinding together beneath oceans. "The Song has been challenged."

Dust swirled up and fled into the trees as Syracuse rose to his full height, blotting out stars as though he had stolen them for himself. Birds screamed in surprise. Three owls spun away, muttering with offended hoots as they abandoned their perch on his spine. The corner of his mouth curved.

"And here I thought," he rumbled with a crooked grin, "that I'd be allowed my nap until the last page was read." The humor thinned quickly, like light through parchment. He lowered his head, and the grin was gone. "The old ones must rise. The quiet ones. The watchers who remember what the world was when it was all chorus and no echo."

He stepped from the cave, and the forest shivered, not in fear, but in relief, as though it had been holding its breath since his last stirring. At the mouth of the cave, a figure waited: a messenger child, hair braided down her back like a river of light. In her small hands, she held a token sealed with fire. It hummed against her palms, making the air taste of cedar and snow.

"For you, Wise One," she said, bowing.

Syracuse bent, claws steady as a surgeon's hand. He broke the seal with his smallest fang and inhaled the fragrance. His nostrils flared.

Light. Heat. A hint of judgment. The faintest memory of incense rising at the Throne.

He closed his good eye and let the meaning fall into him. Then he nodded.

"Understood."

The child smiled, steady now, because the whole world always felt steadier when Syracuse said that.

THE STIRRING OF GRACE AND MERCY

By the River of Life, in a thicket where reeds whispered to each other, two wombat-like creatures stood nose to nose. Their whiskers quivered like harp strings, their ears swiveled like watchtowers. For once, they weren't joking.

Grace sniffed the wind. Her nose wrinkled. "Smell that?"

Mercy tilted his head back, eyes half-shut as if listening to a bell hidden behind mountains. "Feel it, more than smell it. The air's got weight to it. Even the trees are holding their breath."

Grace nodded slowly. "And the river...she's trying not to giggle."

Mercy squinted. "Giggle?"

"Yep. She always giggles when she's nervous. Bubbles too quick. Trips over herself."

Mercy crossed his arms, unimpressed. "You sure that's not you?"

Grace smirked, though her eyes stayed sharp. "Hey, I'm solemn as a stone loaf right now."

The two stared at each other, the silence stretching long enough for a bird overhead to rethink its song. Their mischief never left them, but now it had sunk deep, like lanterns lowered into a well to shine where few could see.

Mercy broke first. "We'd better find Bruce."

Grace snapped her claws against her side. "Or he'll scholar himself straight into a sword fight."

Mercy tried to hide his laugh. "What's the plan?"

"Run fast. Don't trip. And if you see Pride, pretend you're a mirror."

Mercy's mouth opened, then closed again. "That's...actually brilliant."

Grace shrugged, brushing leaves from her fur. "I've been reading Bruce's notes while he naps."

They shared a look, one part fear, one part grin, then darted into the underbrush. Their paws beat a rhythm against the earth. Leaves leapt aside, too respectful to slow them down.

Behind them, the River of Life hiccuped once, as if trying not to laugh at a funeral.

THE CAPTAIN OF THE DEEP

Beneath the Crystal Sea, far below the shimmer where dolphins sketched jokes in spray and angels dove for joy, the deep held its own cathedral. Pressure ruled there, and light was rare and slow. In those caverns, carved before time had a clock, the Captain of the Deep stirred.

His eyes opened first as two lanterns that had not burned in an age. Then his armor shifted, a suit not forged in fire but in the crushing weight where mountains lean against each other. Barnacles clung to his pauldrons like constellations in a private night sky. Veins of bioluminescence traced his chestplate like rivers of blue flame. Kelp wove itself into his bracers, strands swaying as though saluting their master.

When he stood, the sea adjusted. Water groaned like timbers in an ancient ship. Whole reefs leaned toward him, acknowledging the weight of his presence. His voice rolled through the caverns, carried on currents into trenches and through coral cathedrals.

"Summon the host. The time for hiding is over."

At his word, the ocean answered. From the reefs surged rays with spears like sharpened sunbeams. From the trenches rose sharks bearing wide shields, their edges notched with stories of storms they had endured. Barracuda darted in and locked into formation, their flashing bodies snapping into lines as straight as iron. Schools of fish folded together until they formed banners of colors: red, gold, blue; whole sentences in the language of the sea. The ground shook as the whales arrived. Their songs rose like deep brass horns, echoing so powerfully that the seafloor quivered. Each note said the same thing: We have woken.

A small sea-maiden swam near, her hair drifting like living coral, her arms wrapped around a great conch. Her eyes were wide with awe.

"Captain," she said, her voice bubbling like a kettle near the boil, "the surface watches."

"The surface always watches," he replied. His hand, plated in barnacle armor, brushed the conch. "But today the surface waits."

He lifted the conch to his lips. When he blew, the sound was not heard above the waves, but every tide in creation stood still for one heartbeat. Far above, the sea smoothed itself, the waves shivering once as though saluting, then calming flat as polished glass.

The army of the deep had risen.

LIBERTY WATCHES

High above the Kingdom Realm, where the horizon curved like a crown and the clouds lined up as though they were attendants, a shadow passed across the day. The shadow was not absence but authority.

Liberty, the Screaming Eagle of Justice, circled the Place Called Beautiful. Her wings stretched so wide they brushed mountain ridges on one beat and touched the edges of the sea on the next. Each stroke bent the horizon like a bow being drawn. Her eyes, set all around her head, saw everything. She saw what was, and she saw the tremors of what would be. She saw an angel polishing his armor with trembling hands. She saw a council chamber where a map curled under fingers that pressed too hard. She saw a child carrying a scroll, thumb stroking the ribbon twice, as if the parchment itself needed comfort.

Her gaze lingered on the Garden. Even still, even silent, the Garden glowed. Liberty knew it was both the safest place and the most fragile. She angled her wings, riding a current higher, and the air itself sang against her feathers.

A single plume, small and almost invisible, detached from her pinions and drifted downward. When it landed against the city wall, the stone straightened, as if remembering its own vow to hold.

Liberty did not scream. Not yet. Her silence was not weakness; it was mercy dressed in patience. Her scream was a weapon, and weapons wait for their appointed hour.

She sent her thought across the winds, and every loyal heart felt it though they could not have said why:

> I see you. I see your beginning, I see your end. The
> measure will be fair.
> Justice, when it is holy, is mercy's twin wearing
> the robes of a judge.

When she screamed next, the stars themselves would tremble, not from fear, but from recognition.

THE SHADOW COUNCIL

Far from the Dome's pale radiance and the Garden's green hush, another chamber gathered, black as withheld thought, cold as an apology never spoken. Light tried to enter and thought twice. The walls leaned inward, not with welcome, but with hunger. Here, once-loyal beings assembled. Some still glowed faintly at the edges, their loyalty like a cloak slipping from weary shoulders. Others flickered like lamps that had learned to despise oil, light sputtering, ready to extinguish.

At their center stood Sin Say. His smile was a knife polished bright. His hair fell back in a dark river, and when he looked at them, silence itself seemed eager to impress him.

"The Kingdoms prepare," he said, his voice smooth as honey poured over steel. "So must we."

He spread maps across the table. Not maps of rivers or mountains; land obeys boundaries, and he had no patience for obedience. These maps showed currents of influence, territories of fear, regions where loyalty bent under flattery. Lines crisscrossed like spider silk. Curls and notches marked uncertainties, places where questions could grow like weeds.

"Our advantage," Sin Say continued, letting his words coil around the chamber, "is not in numbers. Numbers are for children. Our advantage is in doubt. Doubt multiplies faster than light. Doubt forgets its parents and raises itself."

A figure in the shadows licked dry lips, wings folded so tight he looked like a letter that would never be sent. His voice caught like cloth snagged on a nail.

"And if He speaks? If He says the word? The word that ends this?"

Sin Say leaned close. His smile widened, eyes sharp and strangely human. "He can be doubted," he whispered. "That is enough."

A ripple passed through the chamber, part relief, part dread.

Another voice, younger and eager, piped up. "Shall we strike the Singing Hills? If their songs die first, hope will falter."

Sin Say's eyes narrowed. "Songs do not die. They echo. Kill a hill, and the echo will only grow louder. No..." His hand hovered over the map, a long finger resting where the Dome of Light pulsed faintly. "Strike the memory. Confuse their confidence. Bend the truth until it breaks under its own weight."

A ripple of approval murmured through the chamber. Some nodded, others folded their arms, but none departed. Doubt stitched them tighter than loyalty ever had.

Sin Say rolled the maps closed, his smile slicing across the dark. "The kingdoms prepare their armies. Let them. We will prepare their questions."

The chamber answered with silence, but it was a silence that leaned forward, ready to betray.

THE GATHERING OF THE LEGIONS

Then came the sound that split the stillness. Not brass. Not silver. A trumpet of truth. Its single note raced across mountains, through valleys, into the heart of the Garden. The River of Life leapt against its banks. Lilies lifted their faces. The air itself bent to listen.

And from the four directions, the armies came.

From the East, The Flamebearers. They arrived with torches that revealed rather than burned. The fire they carried showed every shadow for what it truly was. Their commander's face bore scars carved like scripture, each mark a sermon of survival.

"Our task," he told them, "is not to destroy the dark. It is to remind it what light looks like."

From the North, The Swordguard. They marched steady, unhurried, their blades still sheathed, humming softly like rivers under ice. Veterans checked the armor of novices, tugging straps, whispering reminders.

One elder laid a hand on a youth's shoulder. "Mercy strikes wider than anger," she said.

The boy swallowed, nodded, and lifted his chin.

From the West, The Windborne. They came on unseen currents, sometimes touching earth, sometimes vanishing into the clouds. Their wings bent the sky in rhythm, and their bows were strung with air itself. They sang old songs as they flew, songs not heard since the foundations were laid. Birds fell into formation, lending their voices until the whole horizon was music.

From the South, The Watchers of the Deep. The sea split, and its armies rose. Rays carried spears like dawn. Sharks bore shields broad as city gates. Fish folded into banners of color, sentences of motion in the ocean's language. Whales surfaced, their songs booming like cathedral bells underwater. At their center strode the Captain of the Deep, barnacled armor glowing, voice rolling like tides.

"The waters are ready," he said, and the seas obeyed.

THE ASSEMBLY

The four legions gathered at the Throne: east, west, north, and south. Flamebearers, Swordguard, Windborne, Watchers of the Deep. Their commanders bowed low, waiting. Silence returned, heavier than before. The kind of silence that bends knees without command.

THE MARK OF READINESS

And then He came forward.

No crown adorned His brow, no blade hung at His side, yet He radiated a light that dimmed every torch, stilled every wing, silenced every song.

Christian. The Word. The Beginning and the End.

He lifted His hand. Every trumpet ceased, every sword fell still, every wing froze mid-beat. The silence deepened, not the silence of fear but of awe. Even the stars seemed to lean closer, as though waiting for permission to shine again.

And with a voice that had once spoken galaxies into flame, He said, "It is finished."

The words struck deeper than echoes into the marrow of creation itself.

The heavens opened.

Light poured like a river breaking its banks.

And the Battle Before Time began.

CHAPTER TWENTY

The Final Binding

And so the march began. Not of mortal armies, but of realms leaning forward in unison as light against shadow, loyalty against pride. Every wingbeat, every drawn blade of light, every vow unspoken moved toward the center where choice would be tested.

From the brilliance stepped the Holy Advisor, radiant with the presence of the Creator. The legions hushed. Even the shadows stiffened. It was not yet the clash; it was the pause before light and darkness collided, the calm where words still had the power to stay the chains.

ROUND ONE: THE PARLEY

The Advisor's presence carried a gravity that bent silence around him. His robe shimmered with living threads, light woven so deep it seemed to breathe. His eyes searched for Loka, but Sin Say stepped into the foreground first, swagger sharp, his smile a wound that would not close. Behind them stretched two armies, facing one another like tides waiting to break. To the left, legions of flame bore torches that revealed truth in every shadow. To the right, hosts of darkness clutched chains spun from doubt. Wings beat in measured rhythm. Spears glowed. Shields rose. All of creation leaned toward this field, watching the groundless plain between them become a stage.

Sin Say's voice cut the air like a blade. "Stand down, Advisor. Call off your ranks. No chains tighten. Or prove me right that it's always been the Three above all, and the rest of us born to bow."

The Advisor's reply was calm, clear as still water: "I will not trade truth for quiet, nor mercy for fear. Lay down your pride, Sin Say, and none will be bound."

Sin Say's smirk widened. "Then we fight."

The Advisor turned, his voice like steel: "And win we will."

Both commanders wheeled back toward their ranks, and the cosmos trembled with the weight of the decision.

ROUND TWO: THE CLASH OF LEGIONS

A trumpet blast split the heavens. It was not sound alone, but vibration, truth itself shuddering through the fabric of reality. And then the armies moved.

"Legion of the Morning, stand firm!"

"Guardians of the Flame, hold the line!"

"Sentinels of the Dawn, encircle the foe!"

"Hold the Light! Hold the Light!"

Cries erupted like thunder. The battle chant rolled forward in waves, echoing across the realms until mountains quivered and rivers leapt from their beds.

The first collision was like galaxies colliding. Blades of radiant light cut against chains of shadow. Spears of wind bent and snapped against shields of pride. Sea warriors surged from unseen currents, slamming into rebel hosts with the force of tidal waves. Fire-bearers swung torches that revealed lies, and each swing burned shadows into their true shapes.

Immortals cannot die, yet each strike carried binding power. Chains of truth wrapped ankles. Spears of doubt punctured courage. Every blow bound tighter, or loosed freedom. The field became a tapestry of light and dark, woven and torn in the same breath.

Above it all, refrains rang out again and again: "Hold the Light! Hold the Light!"

The stars themselves flickered like candles caught in a storm.

Silence fled; even stillness had joined the battle.

ROUND THREE: THE COUNTERSTRIKE

Then the shadows surged. Loka's voice thundered like a false dawn: "Strike now, and the throne is ours!" His radiance blazed darkly, beauty twisted into pride.

Sin Say roared beside him, his fury echoing the wound of ages. The two advanced together, shoulder to shoulder, pride and bitterness bound like twin storms. Their combined force ripped into the Morning Legion. For a moment, even Michael staggered beneath the blow.

The rebel host howled in triumph. Chains rattled like applause. Shadows swelled, their confidence surging as if victory was at hand.

Angels of flame faltered. Windborne warriors spun out of formation. The tide shifted, if only for a breath. Hope itself trembled.

But across the lines, voices rose again, ragged yet unbroken: "Hold the Light! Hold the Light!"

The chant spread, refusing to die. It threaded through fear, wrapped around courage, and steadied faltering hands. The faithful braced themselves again.

Still, the rebels pressed hard. This was the round where pride looked unstoppable. This was the swing that seemed it could topple heaven.

ROUND FOUR: THE BINDING LIGHT

Then the Creator moved. Not in haste. Not in noise. But in certainty.

Light surged, not from sword or torch, but from the Throne itself. It poured across the battlefield, brilliance so fierce it cast shadows out of existence. From that radiance, bonds began to form, not chains of iron, but chains of mercy and justice, woven together in perfection.

They wrapped around Loka first. He raged, his voice shaking constellations. He strained, wings snapping like banners in a hurricane. But the chains tightened, radiant and unyielding.

Sin Say lunged, eyes blazing with ancient pain. He clawed at the light, trying to wrench it apart, but mercy coiled him too. His scream cut through the heavens, a sound so raw it fractured stars. Still, the chains drew tighter.

And the light did not stop with them.

Across the battlefield, rebel angels found themselves caught in the same torrent. Wings that once gleamed with morning dimmed as radiant bonds seized them. Their beauty twisted as they fought the light, but the chains held fast. Cries and curses rose in a dreadful chorus, thousands bound together in radiant cords.

Then came the casting.

The legions of the fallen, wrapped in light, were hurled down with their leaders. Their screams trailed across the heavens like fire, a torrent of rebellion undone. They fell not into death, for immortals cannot die, but into exile, into the formless void where waters rolled and darkness held sway.

Christian's voice resounded across creation, ancient and mournful: "I saw Satan fall like lightning from heaven."

And so it was.

ROUND FIVE: THE AFTERMATH AND INVITATION

Stillness returned. It was not peace; it was aftermath.

The legions lowered their weapons. Light dimmed back to steady glow. Angels stood shoulder to shoulder, their breaths heavy, their gazes fixed on the place where the rebels had fallen.

Heaven did not rejoice. Justice had been done, but sorrow was heavy. Love had been refused, and eternity bore the scar.

The story was not for them alone. It was a mirror of the battles within every soul. Pride still whispers lies. Bitterness still chains hearts. Fear still says fight instead of forgive. And yet mercy remains, extended again and again, calling us home.

Each of us faces "Loka moments," crossroads where we must choose between surrender and rebellion. The Creator still offers freedom. The same light that bound angels in chains now breaks the chains of human hearts.

If you feel that burden—pride, pain, rebellion—know this: the invitation is for you. Jesus Christ calls you to come as you are, to surrender your struggle, and to step into His light.

Pray, even now, in your own words: "Jesus, I surrender. I turn from my pride and rebellion. Be my Savior. Lead me in Your love and truth. Amen."

The star fell, but redemption still rises. Mercy still waits. The invitation still stands.

CHAPTER TWENTY-ONE

Closing Passage: When a Star Has Fallen

And so the star had fallen.

The heavens fell silent, and the music that once wrapped the realms in wonder was no more.

The Creator did not rise. He sat upon the Throne in perfect stillness, not out of surprise, but as one who already knows the end from the beginning.

Far below, the earth lay formless and void. Waters rolled over a world not yet born. Darkness hovered like a curtain drawn across the stage of history.

There, in that watery deep, the fallen were bound. Chained not by steel, but by the Word.

The silence held its breath. Time itself paused.

For though a star had fallen, the voice that could shatter darkness had only begun to speak.

"Let there be..."

www.ingramcontent.com/pod-product-compliance
Lightning Source LLC
Chambersburg PA
CBHW050454110726
47899CB00003B/940